GHOST TOWN BELLES

Drift Garrity follows a gruelling cowboy life. Working the grub line, poorly paid and without prospects, he determines to unravel the mysteries of the deprived past that has made him what he is. His objective brings him within a trigger-squeeze of death from Macgurie Dan, a reclusive ex-miner who lives a mountain ghost town where he keeps captive his two beautiful daughters, Melissa and Isabella. Also to be tackled is Zack Emmett, vicious range boss and one time gunslick. The trail will lead Drift to dirty tricks, accusations and finally to deadly gunplay amongst the ghost town ruins.

GHOST TOWN BELLES

GHOST TOWN BELLES

by

Chap O'Keefe

Dales Large Print Books
Long Preston, North Yorkshire,
BD23 4ND, England.

British Library Cataloguing in Publication Data.

O'Keefe, Chap
    Ghost town belles.

    A catalogue record of this book is
    available from the British Library

    ISBN   978-1-84262-548-4 pbk

First published in Great Britain in 2006 by Robert Hale Limited

Copyright © Chap O'Keefe 2006

Cover illustration © Gordon Crabb by arrangement with
Alison Eldred

The right of Chap O'Keefe to be identified as the author of this
work has been asserted by him in accordance with the
Copyright, Designs and Patents Act, 1988

Published in Large Print 2008 by arrangement with
Robert Hale Ltd.

Dales Large Print is an imprint of Library Magna Books Ltd.

Printed and bound in Great Britain by
T.J. (International) Ltd., Cornwall, PL28 8RW

1

RIDING THE GRUB LINE

It was coming dark when a lone man, sitting easy in the saddle, came to a fork in the trail. He drew rein and bright, keen eyes studied a rough board nailed to a dead pine. A legend and an arrow had been burned into the sawn wood with a hot iron. 'Broken R' were the words, with the arrow's head indicating the lesser of the two onward routes.

The clopping of hoofs halted, the air was best part silent with the approach of night. Only the incessant crickets chirped. The horse, a black gelding, sensed the rider's apprehension. He threw up his head with a loud jingle of bit-pieces and snorted heavily through distended nostrils.

The rider stroked his lean jaw. 'Well, ol'

hoss, I expect we'll be given the rush again, but we got to give it a try.' Gritted teeth gleamed in a forced grin from his darkly tanned face. 'Every dollar we can make counts.'

Horse and man pressed on.

When they came to it, the inscription's Broken R proved nothing more than two crude, log buildings set against a pine-grown hill and surrounded by a pole fence. It was a pretty spot to live in, but kind of rough to make a good ranch lot. But then the rider had covered a fair expanse of country and he knew the best sites had all been gobbled up long ago by the big outfits that seldom offered what he liked to think of as typical rancher hospitality.

Maybe this place held better promise.

Not that he sought charity. He'd seen enough of what passed for that in a child-hood back East dominated by its untender mercies. No, he was following the time-honoured cowboy custom of riding the grub line.

For most of his kind, end of the fall roundup meant the end of the work year. Fully two-thirds of cowboys he'd known spent the winter working at what jobs they could find in the towns of the West, or doing as he did now – riding from ranch to ranch, looking to get the odd off-season chore, maybe cadging a free meal and a sleep that wasn't to be had rolled in a blanket under the stars.

A horse within the pole corral, but out of sight behind the buildings, sensed the black's approach and whinnied. The rider's bronc pricked up his ears and nickered softly in response. A chestnut mare emerged into the front yard of stomped dirt. The rider hollered.

'Hullo, the house! Anybody home?'

A door swung open, sagging slightly on thick rawhide hinges. A shaft of pale lantern light spilled across the darkening dirt. But none of it spelled a welcome.

The man who came out on to the porch in grey shirt and baggy trousers held up by suspenders clutched a mean-looking double-barrelled shotgun.

'What is it, mister?' he barked. He cocked the gun and pointed it at Drift.

'You Randall?'

'What if I am?'

'They said a ways back you'd mebbe have some work offering. I'm looking for anything that'd tide me over the slack time. Repairs and woodcutting and such'll do me.'

With an aggressive jerk of the shotgun, the rancher cut him off. 'They told yuh wrong, stranger. Who are you?'

'Alexander Garrity's the moniker. Leastways, I was christened Alexander by a ma and pa I never really knew. But the supervisor an' the boys at the Philadelphia orphanage where I spent my childhood called me Drift, on account of I was always running off, it being a harsh place for a freedom-loving sprout to be brung up. Drift has kinda stuck.'

'Well then, mister, *drift* is what it is,'

Randall said sullenly. 'Like I tell all you tumbleweeds – season's over an' I ain't hirin'.'

Drift shook his head regretfully. 'I've ridden awful far, Mr Randall...'

'Sorry, mister – I'm sayin' git, ain't I? Light out. Call on your kinfolks, your friends.'

'Like I said, I ain't got no kin.' Drift assumed his happy-go-lucky manner. 'Nearest thing to kin I got is this here hoss.' He patted the black's neck. 'As for a friend, only one I can trust is my gun.' He let a rawboned hand hover over the black handle of his well-worn Colt .45.

'Make to pull that iron an' I'll cut you in two with buckshot,' Randall growled.

Drift felt his flesh crawl, but laughed. 'Just funning, Mr Randall.'

'Ain't no laughing matter, drifter. All kinds roam through these parts. The fiddle-foot, the renegade, rustlers ... outlaws o' ev'ry stripe. A man cain't be too careful with sich scum a-lookin' to murder him in his bunk, like as not.'

'Laugh kills lonesome,' Drift said, shrugging. He'd had no intention of tangling with Randall or his shotgun. Though handy with a gun, he was not a violent man and harboured no personal resentment of the man.

He'd already noted a brooding suspicion in this neck of the woods and the rancher had as much right to be wary of strangers as any other. In another sparsely populated place, a new face would be welcome. But it seemed hereabouts this was not the case. He couldn't determine the reasons. He knew the country had gone through a gold-rush time some years back. Maybe the roots of it were set in that.

Drift pulled round the head of the black with a tug of the reins. He kneed the weary animal forward at a walk, back in the direction he had come.

'It shouldn't happen to a dog,' he muttered. 'But we ain't a dog: you, hoss, me neither. I'm a cowboy which is maybe worse than a dog.'

He pondered on the trying conditions of his everyday existence. His inherent vagabondage had condemned him to working the grub line – poorly fed and underpaid. When he had a job, he was generally overworked and deprived of sleep. Always he was prone to boredom and loneliness.

It was no wonder few cowboys lasted but seven-some years on the range before seeking out a more human and settled existence in the townships. The calling that led a fellow to become a cowboy was seldom romantic. The life attracted young men without family, property or other work opportunities.

Drift could stomach the deprivations while he was young; still fit and uncrippled or maimed by the all-too-frequent work accidents. The roping and branding of cattle ate up all a man could supply in wit, strength and nerve. Broken limbs and lost fingers were commonplace, and though standing tall and broad-shouldered today, he knew he wouldn't always be tough and indestructible.

Before his prime was over, he wanted to solve the mystery that had made him what he was; possibly to settle an account. The mission had led him to these parts, and it would take more than the discouragement of a surly rancher before he'd quit them.

Down the main trail apiece from the dead pine and its Broken R marker, Drift ended his day's riding as full dark closed in. He would wait for daylight before returning to the last plains township, Two Springs. The black needed rest before being pushed hard again, and with no moon yet risen the un-familiar trail could be dangerous anyway.

He found a place where he could make camp and undid the black's saddle cinches, concentrating his troubled mind and energy on the mundane routine now necessary. He offloaded the saddle, blanket, bedroll and the rest of his gear. Then he led the horse to a small stream nearby. After letting him drink his fill, he led him back to where the grazing grass was thick and picketed him on a long rein.

Untying his bedroll, Drift spread his black oilskin slicker on the ground beside the saddle. Though the weather had long been dry, a damp chill was rising in the hollow. Maybe it was from the stream. He dumped his blankets on the slicker and built a small fire from gathered dead wood.

Before long he was sitting on his blankets, looking into the glowing embers of the fire, with a scratch but hot meal glowing comfortably under his belt and a tin cup of hot coffee in his hands.

At length, he threw the dregs into the fire. He yawned and stretched, wrapped himself in the blanket, and settled his head on the seat of the saddle for a pillow.

He didn't plan on letting disgruntlement at being seen off by Randall work on his temper. He was well versed over many years in saving his ingrained bitterness for another matter. Tomorrow would be time enough for resuming the hunt to straighten out his unsettled life, to still the demons that had made him what he was. And he planned to get an early start on hieing him back to Two Springs.

Five minutes later he was snoring gently, dead to the world.

He woke before dawn, rekindled his fire and made a scant meal of coffee, a slice of ham and hard biscuits dunked in the coffee. He carried his two canteens down to the stream and filled them before saddling and loading the black.

Despite his prompt rising, the sun was well up in the sky when Drift and his black shambled dispiritedly into the dusty main street of Two Springs. But ragged clouds veiled the brightness from time to time, foretelling a coming of cooler days and maybe rains.

Two Springs was a buoyant if not prosperous settlement. Horsemen and rigs passed to and fro. The boardwalks carried a steady traffic of people – men, women and youths. The town was a sprawl of buildings that seemed to have been constructed at random, with no thought for design or plan.

A typical, quarter-mile long cow-town that would have sprung up round a cattle trail fifteen or twenty years back, Two Springs now had some establishments that were substantial, like the new-looking, stone-built branch of the territorial bank and the courthouse with adjoining law office and jail. What remained of the huddle of original shacks and clapboard buildings was being crowded out. Where not much rebuilding had taken place, like at Gruber's Saloon, false fronts had been added.

Drift rode past a cross street steadily creeping toward the new rail depot. New buildings were under construction, further changing the face of Two Springs.

He thought how little there was to show of the town's reputedly troubled past. First, it had been Indians; later, one range war after another; then, a gold-rush crowd had rampaged through on its way to nearby mountains. A year ago, track-laying gangs had regularly brawled among themselves or with range hands in town on drinking sprees.

Suddenly, as though cued by his thoughts of bygone turmoil, the peaceful street scene was torn apart by pandemonium. The slamming of a door and an almighty metallic clatter behind him had Drift swinging round in his saddle.

A short ways along the street, a young woman had burst out from Jennings's Mercantile, the biggest of the Two Springs general stores. Barnaby Jennings sold just about everything of a non-specialist nature from basic groceries to zinc bathtubs. It was a stack of the latter, displayed beside the entrance, that the girl had tipped over after slamming shut the store door behind her.

Her disruptive actions appeared deliberate. And there was no accident about how she leaped from the boardwalk and began running up the street fast and nimble as a hare.

Drift jerked the black to a halt. He saw that the girl – she looked as though she might have known sixteen summers – was unusual, wild. She was barefoot and had long black hair that flew like a banner in the wind behind her. She was dressed in a fringed coat and skirt of doeskin. Both were old and streaked with dirt and stains; both were short, the skirt almost indecently so by the standards of the day. The tattered hemline was closer to her knees than her ankles and uneven.

In one hand she clutched what looked like a brilliant red neckerchief, unfaded by the sun and straight from the store shelf with a price ticket attached.

Before she'd run more than a few paces, the store's door was flung open again. The beefy storekeeper, Jennings, cheeks red above his longhorn moustache, charged out still in the apron he customarily removed before venturing from his premises.

In his hand was a massive Walker Colt revolver, fifteen and a half inches long. He raised the powerful weapon and aligned the sights – one on a blade near the end of the barrel and one notched in the hammer. The muzzle snarled flame visible in the sunlight.

The shot kicked up dust alongside the wild girl's flashing feet. She faltered, hopping as though her feet had been stung, to an uncertain stop.

'Stop, thief!' Jennings roared. 'Or I'll shoot again and not to miss!' He pointed the gun again at the terrified girl. Drift heard the hammer click.

The street had miraculously emptied. Folks in Two Springs knew their guns and didn't want to be anywhere around. The storekeeper's .44 pistol was of a type recognized throughout the West since the 1840s to be as effective as a common rifle at one hundred yards and better than a musket even at two hundred.

Drift slid from his saddle, dismounting cautiously but speedily despite a certain stiffness from his long ride. He hitched to a nearby rail. Watched.

Jennings strode after the girl who backed up against an awning post at the side of the street. Seeing he had her at his mercy, he uncocked and turned the weighty gun. He blew down the barrel. A drift of blue gunsmoke passed across his smug face.

Reaching the girl, he stuffed the gun into the top of his trousers where it was partly concealed by the apron. He raised his other hand as though to cuff the girl. She cringed.

Drift rapped, 'You don't have to do that!'

He moved in closer.

Surprised by the intervention, Jennings's eyes switched toward him. They narrowed, hostile and calculating. Drift saw two deep scores made angry tracks on the store-keeper's left cheek. Had he been scratched?

'What's this to you, sticky beak?' Jennings demanded, but lowered his hand. 'The wildcat robbed the store. Look! She's got the evidence in her hand – that silk necker-chief.'

Freed from the fear of a punishing slap, the girl straightened up. Her black hair hung in tangled locks about her face and neck; her dusky-skinned face flushed with the stress of her laboured breathing. She had a short, straight nose, beaded with perspiration, and black flashing eyes.

'He lies!' she spat. 'He gave me neckerchief in exchange for a kiss. But he want more. He put his hand up my skirt. I try to scratch his eyes out. Then I run.'

'Hogs' swill!' Jennings said. 'She'll get what's coming to her. Gals like her do, sooner or later.'

'The facts of it should be heard according to law,' Drift said. 'It ain't right to fight a girl, even a thief, with a gun.'

Hard anger stiffened the storekeeper's bulky frame and darkened his face. He snarled, 'You're making a mistake, mister, horn–'

He never finished because a third party took an unexpected hand in the simmering row.

Across the street was a barbershop. From it erupted an old-timer, fresh from the interrupted luxury of a 'boughten' shave. His whiskery face was half-lathered and half-shaven. A towel billowed from his shoulders like a cloak.

From the plankwalk, he bellowed, 'Yuh leave m' daughter be, yuh dirty varmints!'

Jennings shouted, 'Shut your squawking, you old fool!'

The barber's agitated customer teetered on the edge of the walk precariously, then jumped down beside an ancient buckboard to which was hitched a brace of fly-bitten and decrepit mules.

The barber hovered on the threshold of his shop, soap-dripping razor yet in hand.

'Hold your horses, Dan!'

But the old-timer did no such thing. All in a trice, he grabbed a carbine, an old 1866 model Henry, from under a tarp on the ramshackle rig, and promptly whipped it to his shoulder. Taking snap aim, he squeezed the trigger.

Drift was agape and helpless.

The gun roared and the crescent butt plate bucked against the old man's towelled shoulder.

2

MAYHEM ON MAIN STREET

Drift felt the wind of the .44 slug as it passed between himself and Jennings. That was too damned close.

The storekeeper backed off in terror. 'Now you've done it, you interfering bastard!' he rapped at Drift. 'It's Melissa's pa – Mad Dungaree Dan!'

'*I've* done it...!' Drift was incredulous, but while Jennings retreated, he stood his ground.

The old-timer kept advancing. This Mad Dungaree Dan did indeed wear faded bib-overalls of studded denim. He also had piercing eyes that glinted like a hawk's from a seamed and leathery face.

When he abruptly levered the carbine,

Drift closed in on him. The weapon was the model that had been dubbed the Yellowboy for its bright brass frame, but the metal on Mad Dan's example was tarnished to a dull brown. Even so, it was demonstrably in working order, and Drift didn't figure on letting him use it again. He had no way of knowing at whom or what the crazy old man intended to shoot.

'Don't be hasty, old-timer,' he said. 'There's been a misunderstanding. Drop the Henry. You wouldn't want to die.'

'Me die!' Mad Dan cackled. He was close enough now for Drift to smell his foul breath, which surely must have made the barber nauseous. In his mouth were but four rotten teeth. 'Yuh talk mighty brave for a driftin' cowpoke. Yuh'll make the fifth man I've blown t' hell for a-pesterin' m' gals.'

He levelled the Henry and wrapped his finger round the trigger.

Drift feinted to the right, knowing that at close quarters, the carbine's bullet would blast a gruesomely fatal hole though his belly. But when the weapon roared again, it was pointing skywards and Drift was wresting it from Mad Dan's grasp.

Drift's forward lunge had been faster than a striking rattler's and the disarming was over before the few hiding spectators close enough to see at all could witness its efficiency: a seizing of the gun, a planting of a cowboy boot over Mad Dan's instep, a hefty shove.

Drift's boots had a high arched vamp, two-inch heels and thin soles to give him the feel of the stirrup. The heels were designed to prevent the foot slipping through the stirrup and were attached securely enough to serve as a brace when roping on foot.

When Drift freed Mad Dan's trapped foot from under his own, the Henry was in his hands.

The old man staggered back a step or two from Drift's vicious push. A spasm of rage and frustration contorted his lined features.

'Sonofabitch!' he hissed. 'Yuh're stickin' your neck out, boy – thar'll be a reckonin' fer this!'

Drift suspected he might have caught a tiger by the tail. What he didn't expect was swift retribution by the tiger's cub. All at once, a hail of stinging blows descended on his back and shoulders.

'You better let Pa alone!' the wild girl screeched. 'Lay hands on him and you be kilt!'

'Hey! You, too, lost your brains, girl? I ain't–'

But the girl wasn't listening to Drift's explanations. She'd seemingly forgotten the favour he'd done her in rescuing her from the dirty clutches of the storekeeper who'd called her Melissa. She went right on pummelling him with bunched little fists and kicking at him with unexpectedly hard and rigid bare feet.

The blows, though a girl's, hurt. Drift shook his head exasperatedly. With the carbine still in his hands, what was he to do? Drop it? Hit back at her? Try to hold her?

He was in a hell of a bind. He wasn't the

sort of man to fell a female with his fists – even if she was a spitfire. Townsfolk were returning to the street, not to continue about their everyday affairs, but to stand and be amused.

When a set of fingernails raked his cheek, Drift decided enough was enough. For a start, he relinquished his hold on the carbine. It proved the best and the worst thing to do.

Melissa broke off her assault immediately. But what Drift hadn't realized, his eyes half-closed in instinctive protection from her nails, was that one of her hands had already closed around the midpoint of the gun's nineteen-inch barrel.

When he released his clutch, the carbine went fully into Melissa's grasp. Instantly she skipped away, laughing. 'I got gun, Pa! We go!'

Drift shook his head, bemused. Onlookers who'd emerged from cover laughed jeer-ingly. But their mirth was short-lived. For the girl handed the carbine to her aged parent who presented and swung it menacingly. A second time, the street cleared in short order.

The bizarre pair clambered on to their buckboard. Drift caught a flicker of lithe brown thigh as Melissa's short skirt rode up her bare legs. On board, she took up the reins and a whip from a bracket.

Mad Dan cried, 'Feed the critters leather, M'liss!'

She lashed at the backs of the mules, who'd been dozing unconcernedly, and they surged into their collars, braying in indignation and long ears laid back. The rig's wheels churned up a mighty cloud of dust.

Mad Dan stood in the swaying buckboard's tray, legs spread and back braced against the seat. He levered the carbine rapidly, firing off street-sweeping shots.

Alarmed horses at hitch rails bucked, letting fly hind legs in fierce kicks, snorting through flared nostrils. Two tore free and reared up, pawing the air before they went pounding down the street in the opposite direction to the buckboard, broken reins flying, teeth bared in fright and anger.

One of Mad Dan's bullets took out the window of a room above Jennings's store, the glass imploding with a crash. Drift couldn't tell whether this was purposeful or accidental, but by the time the buckboard had hurtled past the main street's limits, with the mules whipped up into a frantic burst of speed, he reckoned Mad Dan must have emptied the magazine.

Hoofbeats and the unstable buckboard's rattling died into the distance. The banner of dust grew smaller and smaller till it vanished in the direction of the foothills lining the western horizon.

Slowly, subtly, the town came back to life. Men and women appeared yet again on the sidewalks.

And Barnaby Jennings confronted Drift.

'Say, cowboy,' he said, all aggression, 'you let that teasing little bitch leave with unpaid-for goods!'

Drift looked around, and scoffed. 'Now

you mention it, guess she has took the pretty red neckerchief with her – but they left us with our lives, didn't they? Ain't you being kind of ungrateful?'

'The young hellion dented some ten-dollar baths to boot. I got a business to run. There was no call for you to shove your oar in. What are you going to do about it?'

Drift studied the storekeeper with contempt. 'I ain't about to go fondle her ass, mister, that's for sure.'

Jennings flushed guiltily, then bristled. 'Are you making allegations?'

Drift wanted no part of it. He shrugged. 'What say I foot the bill for the item the young lady forgot to pay for, friend? I don't like to be associated with petty disputes, or bad feelings.'

Jennings demanded two dollars. Though Drift could have sworn the tag on the colourful silk neckerchief had said $1.50, and he could ill-afford extra expense, he handed over the sum uncomplainingly.

Avid eavesdroppers on the transaction

sniggered delightedly. A group of cowhands on the overlooking boardwalk even raised a mocking cheer and a clap or two.

Jennings snapped, 'Quieten down, you idiots! This ain't none of the Box V's concern.'

Which only prompted another howl of derisive laughter.

Jennings gave a disgusted snort, turned heel and stamped back to his store. Drift shrugged and went to reassure his edgy black.

Drift pushed slowly through the batwing doors into Gruber's Saloon, pausing momentarily once inside to let his eyes become accustomed to the indoors after the bright sunlight. The room was no different from many he'd seen, all dark wood and tobacco-browned wallpaper with sawdust on the floor.

A hush fell when he was observed, but the buzz of conversation resumed quickly. Patrons who'd seen the fracas on the street earlier were none too discreet in tipping off their companions about the salty newcomer to town.

Drift walked slowly forward to the counter, lifting one foot to rest on the brass footrail that ran along its front. He pushed up his hat till it was loose on his head and smiled at one of the two men tending the bar. From his previous passing through Two Springs, he knew this was Wes Gruber, owner of the saloon.

Gruber was a fat man with a flabby, heavily jowled face and cold, washed-out eyes that had yellowed whites. He eyed Drift sardonically across the counter, one hand resting on a damp and grey, tatty-edged bar cloth.

'What'll it be, stranger?' he asked.

'Whiskey ... and I'd appreciate your local knowledge, if you've got the time.'

Gruber turned to reach behind, then slid bottle and glass across the counter and waved a hand in invitation. 'Have one on the house, and put your questions,' he said.

'Thank you kindly,' Drift said. 'One, I'm looking for work, and two, I'd be obliged to know more about an old man they call Mad Dungaree Dan.'

Gruber frowned. 'Grub-line rider, huh? The outfits in this neck of the woods will all tell you the same – they ain't hiring. I figger you've heard that yourself. As for the other, there's more rumours than you could put salt on the tail of in a coon's age.'

'Do tell,' Drift encouraged. He noticed, too, that a bunch of cowhands he'd seen previously on a boardwalk at the time of his clash with Jennings were nudging one another and bending a listening ear in the bar's direction. He wondered at their interest; also, at their hamfisted attempts to conceal it with exaggerated preoccupation elsewhere.

Gruber stuck a finger in his ear and twisted it thoughtfully.

'Fact of the matter is, the old man is a kind of legend. He came as a miner in the territory's gold rush. A real ornery jasper. Stayed up on the mountain after the find was played out and Highgrade Pocket became a ghost town. Him and his two girls are the Pocket's last inhabitants.'

The saloon man paused to wipe his finger on the wet bar cloth.

'Girls?' Drift said. 'You mean, he has more than the one daughter.'

'Yeah, two – Melissa and Isabella – M'liss and Issy. The ghost town belles, the bravos call 'em, though not to their father's face.'

'They have – er – friends in Two Springs?'

Gruber laughed. 'Naw! Far from it. They're sort of untouchable, on account of their crazy pa. Issy the elder's a right handsome piece but a soft-brain, it's been put about. Mad Dan keeps 'em both up there on the mountain in seclusion, under the protection of his gun. He values privacy above all else and he's a mighty fine shot with a rifle. Handy with a knife likewise. They say he's done for three or four who've gone sniffing after his beautiful girls.'

The bunch of cowhands – four of them – shuffled closer to the counter.

'Come on, you *hombres*, step up to the bar,' one said. 'All drinks are on Lew. Set 'em up, Wes!'

'What's this, Feffer?' Gruber asked.

Drift, out of the corner of his eye, caught the quick wink the man called Lew gave the man behind the counter.

'My birthday,' Lew said. 'Bottles and glasses for everyone. And fill the stranger's glass here, too.'

Lew was a beanpole-lean, black-bearded man in patched Levis and a scuffed leather vest over a plaid work shirt, longsleeved but collarless.

Drift figured he was being set up, though for what he didn't know. Maybe these roosters thought he was a sucker. They were among those who'd followed what had gone down outside between Melissa, the storekeeper, himself and Mad Dungaree Dan. They'd probably seen how he'd meekly paid off Jennings to keep the peace and thought he'd be easy to separate from what was keeping him from being totally broke. He hoped they didn't think he'd come full-handed rather than half-shod.

Drift's guess started to prove right when Lew Feffer produced a deck of cards and suggested the party should retreat to a corner table for a little sport.

'Nothing to strain the brain – let us boys unlimber for a little three-card monte among friends.'

Lew's pals were good-heartedly vociferous in approving the suggestion.

In Drift's experience, frontier gambling took two forms: games of chance and confidence games. The latter were scarcely games at all, but swindles that included variations of thimble rig, the old shell game – and three-card monte.

Which of the three face-down cards was the queen? The gullible contestant who placed a bet had almost no chance of winning, but Drift decided he'd buy it.

He'd play dumb and go along for a while, to see what panned out.

3

DRIFT PLAYS CARDS

Mad Dungaree Dan's rattletrap buckboard, jouncing along at a more sedate pace – one less likely to bust its protesting axles or exhaust the two ageing mules – climbed away from the plains into the foothills.

Ahead lay the high mountains and great forests where wild game roamed, and Melissa and Isabella her sister lived in isolation with their possessive father in the ghost town called Highgrade Pocket.

Melissa looked back regretfully at the shrinking conglomeration of 'living' buildings that made up the thriving ranch town of Two Springs. The land, too, was good there – fertile and beautiful, the lush grasslands dotted with the herds of men's cattle beasts.

It was a shame the storekeeper Jennings had touched her in a way she knew he shouldn't. Entirely unaccustomed to human society and civilization, she found the town fascinating; so tidy compared to the rotting structures she was familiar with at High-grade Pocket and, being the resort of rough-and-tumble cowboys and cowmen, full of interesting people of which her life was devoid.

Once, her pa had taken both M'liss and Issy into the town on a Sunday. Afterward, he'd said it had been a big mistake and vowed and declared he would never do it again.

Sunday was apparently the big day in Two Springs. As well as roistering cowboys, the Sabbath there had included such activities as horse racing, cockfighting, preaching, a wedding and a general fandango at a large dance hall. Melissa had never seen the likes.

She wondered if her sadly long-departed mother, Consuela, had known similar scenes in her native Mexico, a land that seemed impossibly far away, very foreign and spoken of by her pa only in derogatory terms.

Late in the evening, a bunch of range riders hurrahed Two Springs. They rode fast down the main street, merrily whooping. Arriving outside Gruber's Saloon in a cloud of dust orangey-brown in the lamps' light, they blazed off guns into the air, yelling shrilly and raucously in celebration of what Melissa saw only as their high spirits.

They also seemed to think they were pretty special and could do anything they wished, like the kings and lords in the simple story books Issy sometimes haltingly read her.

But then what was an exciting, amusing spectacle turned frightening.

When they jumped from their horses, two of the riders cornered Issy, who was two years older than Melissa and in looks fairer and more North American. They pawed at her clothing till her father arrived and shot one of them.

Pa said they were going to rape Issy, which meant they would mate with her, as M'liss

40

had seen only animals do, spying on them in their secret places in the mountain timberlands. But this mating in the dust of the open street would have been forceful and wicked.

The loud-mouthed cowboys had also poked fun at the three of them for their strange clothes and called Issy a 'soft-brain'. Pa had never taken Issy to Two Springs again, nor ever visited on a Sunday.

But these days, she knew, Pa himself would often lie with Issy and do things that she knew were not in accordance with the world of nature that made up her everyday surroundings. Thus grudging respect for her father was tempered with the untaught conviction that the way he treated Issy, if not herself, was wrong.

Melissa heaved a great sigh. Life was a great mystery and very complicated, it seemed.

She wondered if all cowboys and townsmen were as bad as her pa stated. Today, she had liked the looks of the young man who'd rescued her from the vile Jennings. It all seemed mighty silly, but her thoughts often turned to the mating thing of late. She wondered if one day she might find that handsome cowboy again, and be allowed to dance with him and, yes, mate with him, as the birds and other creatures of the wild – elk and deer, bobcat and black bear – did so prolifically and seemingly pleasurably.

No, of course not ... Pa would forbid it.

Her father, now driving their creaking conveyance, said brusquely, 'Quit your day-dreamin', M'liss. I do b'lieve yuh're gettin' quite listless in your ways. Mebbe town don't agree with your constitooshun.'

Drift's mind was not wholly on the cards. He pondered the story of the reclusive Mad Dungaree Dan and the speculation and lusting that surrounded his allegedly captive daughters.

The gold rush link had a significance to him and he would have to make further investigations. It was reason enough to stay in this country for a spell, find work to support himself, make friends...

His companions had launched into the opening rounds of the game that Drift knew wasn't a game, and his distracted manner was beginning to draw curious stares. Making an effort, he concentrated his attention on the cards.

He also strived not to disabuse them of their belief that he was wet behind the ears.

Lew Farrer had taken on the role of the tosser or dealer. He manipulated the cards with long, dexterous fingers, and took the bets. It was plain to Drift that Lew's pards – they all rode for a Box V spread – were working with him as a team, doing the job of being his shills, or accomplices.

The object of the game was simple. Lew had three cards, one of which was a queen. They were shown to the others gathered round and then thrown facedown on the table. Lew invited the players to bet on which card was the queen.

In round after round, Lew's pals picked the right card and won the money. Drift couldn't spot how it was done. Sleight of hand? Marked cards? Whatever, he was being given the clear impression that the 'house', Lew, could be beaten. Their plan, he suspected, was to tempt him into the game with bets of his own. First, they'd let him win a few deals no doubt. Later, they'd raise the stakes and take back everything he'd won and more.

Tentatively, when in good faith he could delay his move no longer, he placed a bet. And won the money.

Lew's bunch cheered and slapped him on the back.

'The luck's with yuh, Drift!'

'Try ag'in!'

Drift did. And he put in extra money from his pocket, to firm up their notion that he was hooked.

Once more, he won, and Lew swore. 'How come you got all the luck?'

'Clean living, I guess,' Drift joked.

The third time, Lew refused Drift's bet on the grounds he could accept only one bet at a time and one of the others had beaten him to it.

This, Drift thought, was a lie, designed to make him bet even higher and faster in the next round.

A stubbly-faced hand by the name of Pete nudged him in the back and whispered, 'Aw, yuh'll be in an' winning next time. Lew's kinda uppity, since he knows yuh're on a winning streak. We'll give yuh some help. Watch real close.'

At the end of the round, the accepted gambler diverted Lew's attention while collecting his winnings. Pete swiftly reached forward and bent the corner of the queen.

'Yuh'll have nothin' to worry 'bout now,' he mumbled under his breath.

Drift figured the Box V crew, all in cahoots with Lew, was moving in for the kill. Somehow the card that had been marked for him as the queen was going to be switched with another. The contest was between his eyes and Lew's lightning-fast long fingers. Maybe the bent card would be unbent and another bent in its stead. Maybe a fourth card would be substituted from Lew's long sleeves.

Drift didn't want to know. He'd seen such tricks played in other places, and he wasn't as green as they thought he was. He knew he'd stuck his neck out far enough.

'Well, that was damn' good fun, gents, but if you'll excuse me, I reckon I should quit while I'm ahead. Thanks for the winnings.'

He looked around him, sweeping the room with a searching gaze. 'Now where's the privy in this joint?'

Brushing off the company's protests – its adamancy that he was about to reap a minor fortune – and insisting on the urgency of answering the call of nature, Drift headed for a door at the rear of the smoky room.

He chuckled to himself as he took a backyard walk that meandered past stacks of empty crates and several open sacks of fly-infested garbage to an outhouse with an unpainted, sun-warped door.

'Fooled the foolers!' he triumphed quietly in its musty interior.

4

THE ANGRY RANGE BOSS

When Drift returned to the saloon, he went straight to the counter, warily avoiding his new 'friends' and ordering a new bottle and glass.

Lew and his bunch seemed to have forgotten him already, thank God, and were deeply involved in earnest conversation. That was just dandy by Drift. He didn't want to buy into any more fights in Two Springs. But moments later his ears pricked up as their voices were raised.

'I tell yuh, Lew, I've about had it up to here with the amount o' work Big Dutch is pilin' on our plates.'

'True,' put in Pete, rasping his rough chin between finger and thumb. 'Mebbe the boss should hire on more hands 'tween now an' the spring roundup. There's chores fer a whole army on the Box V.'

'Tell your grizzles to Zack Emmett, not me,' said Lew. 'He's Van Dam's range boss, ain't he?'

More was said along similar lines, but in the hubbub of other saloon give-and-take, Drift was unable to catch all the details.

Hmmm ... Drift thought. This sounds mighty interesting; a lot more so than those jiggers' three-card monte stunt. Maybe without realizing it they've done me a favour after all.

A little later, Wes Gruber pushed his disreputable bar cloth along the counter, mopping up slops, and Drift was able to call on him again as a source of information.

'Box V is Big Dutch's spread, richest and biggest for a hundred miles around,' the saloon owner said.

'Big Dutch?'

'Yeah. A Dutchman, Kiliaen Van Dam. He inherited the original holding from his pa, the first Big Dutch, and built on it. A powerful man. Blunt and unyielding. No one messes with Big Dutch, or his range boss, Zachary Emmett.'

'So it's Emmett who runs the outfit, day to day?'

'Sure. And a mean piece of work, Emmett. They say he was hired on first for his prowess as a gunhand in range-war days. When a tough *hombre* like him works for a top cattleman like Big Dutch – and looks out for his interests – you got a considerable combination.'

Gruber leaned his aproned bulk over his side of the counter. He said in confidential tones, 'No one bucks the Box V. Now Emmett's cock of the roost, and they do say with ambitions to marry Big Dutch's daughter and heir, Rebecca.'

It was enough for Drift to know, and as much as he was to learn. A customer hammered an empty bottle on the counter top and threw down coins. For Gruber, chinwag with a passing cowhand who looked nigh on broke lost its attraction. Gruber went along the bar to serve him.

Next day, after Drift had been turned down for a job at the livery stable, he left town with directions to the Box V. It sounded like the brand had no shortage of money and needed more hands. All he had to do was make a pitch that would persuade them to outlay the chickenfeed it would take to hire him on.

It was an axiom with Drift that a grub-line rider never knew what the next turn of the trail would bring to him. This day, several hours' riding out of Two Springs, negotiating a rocky outcrop, it was a big sign erected on a lumber arch over the roadway. The sign said:

BOX V RANCH. KEEP OUT.
TAKE NOTE – THIS MEANS YOU.
KILIAEN VAN DAM, OWNER.

A stab of unease went through Drift, but he ignored the prohibition. He rode on.

50

The trail inside the Box V boundary skirted through the foothills of the mountain range that marked the western reaches of the vast property. When the way climbed to a ridge in the rolling terrain, Drift pulled the black to a halt and surveyed the land from his vantage point, senses alert for any movement, any sound.

Twisting in the saddle, he looked back in the direction he had come and his keen eyes spied a covered wagon drawn up in a swale likely low enough to carry water during heavy rainstorms. Thus, it had previously been hidden from him.

Men, some four or five, appeared to be repairing a break in a fence there that closed off the deepest bottom of the swale, a place likely to be precariously boggy at times of the year.

Drift had done his share of hauling stuck cows out of such hell's half-acres, having often obeyed orders 'to ride bog and tail 'em up'. He could understand the purpose and worth of these men's work. The rig was probably their chuck and supply wagon. Drift decided he would do his cause no harm by approaching the party.

He lost no time in riding down over the grass toward the men. Sign became apparent that at some time recently a few head of stock had been driven through the swale, demolishing the fence. As he approached, a tall, granite-faced gent in his late thirties, all angles and whipcord muscle, pushed away from one of the wagon's wheels where he'd been leaning hipshot, taking his time building a smoke.

Drift noted he wore two walnut-gripped .45s thonged low on his thighs in deep-cut holsters and that he was suddenly all hostile attention.

'Who the hell are you?' he clipped. 'Didn't you read the sign over the trail? Get out!'

Drift saw no sense in not saying his piece, having ridden this far. He dismounted.

'I'm Drift Garrity, and I sure read the sign.'

He continued on a hunch he'd formed

about the man's identity. 'You Zachary Emmett, foreman of the Box V? I heard you were short a couple of men. Well, I'm a broke cowhand, and I'd admire to have a job hereabouts.'

'After fall and with cattle prices dropping? Hah hah! Funny man, huh? When you get through laughin', get ridin'!'

Drift gave a friendly grin. 'Well, you sure look like you could do with some laughs in your day. Don't mean no disrespect. Nor do I see I done anything wrong.'

Along about then, Drift noticed that among the hands who'd been wrestling new fence posts into deep holes were Lew Feffer and his sidekick Pete. Both were smirking.

Drift knew in the same instant he'd been had.

There were no vacancies on the Box V payroll. It was just another con – a payback by the peeved hands whose three-card monte had failed to cheat him of his residual dinero, to which he'd actually added a mite at their expense.

Drift also apprehended that Zack Emmett was a real tough customer, surly and dangerous, and his (Drift's) nerve to trespass in defiance of Kiliaen Van Dam's sign had gotten him riled. His challenging lip was the last straw.

Emmett's weathered face congested with rage. 'By God, you done everythin' wrong! You're gonna be broken as well as broke, kid.'

His big right fist swung.

Drift was nothing if not agile on his feet, but directly from the saddle, he was also stiff. The blow caught the side of his ducking head above the left ear. He was knocked violently sideways and a shower of stars exploded in his head like a fire-work. He managed, though, to keep his footing, and shaking his head to clear his blurred vision, he saw Emmett's thin, evil smile at the result of his handiwork.

He vowed to himself he'd wipe that unholy smile off the ugly face.

Quick as light, Drift danced in, fists raised,

ready to do battle. He saw the surprised range boss sidestep, and the blind fury well up in him at the drifter's audacity.

Emmett threw another poleaxing punch, but it went over Drift's head. Evading the mighty, rock-hard fist, Drift went low and got in two strong body punches. He felt his bunched knuckles sink a smidgen into Emmett's solar plexus, evincing sharp gasps of pain from the man and sending him staggering back.

But the respite was only momentary. Emmett came back roaring, his blood up, his eyes glinting fiercely.

'Flatten the bastard, Zack!' Lew Feffer howled.

Drift backed off on to what he thought was clear, level ground where he'd have room to manoeuvre. This fight had to be defensive as well as offensive. He was risking his life, taking on so efficient and ruthless opponent. The only weak point was Emmett's sense-sapping anger.

A combination of two basic errors nearly

undid Drift. The ground he backed on to was not as even as he'd supposed, and he failed to avoid a blow which, though it missed his face, slammed into his shoulder just as his heel lodged in a hole underfoot. Next moment, the two men had crashed to the ground, arms and legs thrashing wildly.

Drift fought with a savage, ferocious determination. He tasted blood in his mouth as the flesh inside was crushed against his own teeth. He knew he had to get to his feet first. If Emmett beat him to it, he'd no doubt he'd be dealt brutal kicks and a possibly fatal stomping under the thuggish man's boots.

Using what purchase he could find with an elbow, buttock and heel, and by dint of all the might he could muster, Drift rolled, forcing Emmett over sideways and off his tortured body.

Drift went up on hands and knees and scrambled upright not a moment too soon. Emmett was also up and still ready to slug away till he put Drift down for good. His eyes purely gleamed with vicious hate.

The young cowboy retreated from the flailing fists, dodging the worst of the punishment. He angled round so he had the wagon at his back. No sooner had Drift's shoulders hit the wagon than Emmett lunged in with a punch that would have crushed his head against the wagon's side had it landed.

But Drift was using the brains inside his ringing head. He was dodging the fist even as it began its powerful swing. Emmett's hand cracked against the lumber making the entire wagon rock and bringing forth from his throat a yell of excruciating agony.

And in that moment Drift began the sally that would wrap up the fight or, if it failed, seal his doom.

First, a hammer blow to Emmett's ribs, then as Emmett's head came down, a right-hander that took him solidly on the side of the jaw, its velocity augmented by the force of the man's own doubling-over.

Emmett's mouth sagged open, and Drift followed up his sudden advantage, pursuing him as he tottered backwards limply, almost in slow motion. The power in Emmett's punches was sapped now, and Drift could hit him almost at will. Through the fog of his own pain, he delivered more blows, each one jarring him from his sore knuckles to his toes.

A sweeping right to the face; a left to the heart; a right to the mid-section. Drift put every ounce of strength he still had into making his calculated punches count.

With the fourth hit, under the bracket of the chin, Emmett was finally lifted up on his toes, and they could have been lifted off the ground. His eyes went glassy, and he was dumped sprawling on his back in the dust, senseless. Drool and blood trickled from the corner of his mouth.

Drift stood over him – swaying, panting, dripping sweat. It had been a hell of a fight. He couldn't remember being in a scrap much worse, ever. He ached all over. His left eye was swollen and threatening to close up. But when he saw Emmett wasn't going to get up in a hurry, he forced himself to straighten and draw in a deep, steadying breath.

He blew on a bruised and bleeding hand, flexed the fingers and said, 'I only came to make a reasonable enquiry. A civil response would've been a whole lot easier.'

But he was wrong if he thought the trouble was over. Lew Feffer had edged to the wagon, from where he grabbed up a shotgun that belonged to the crew's cook.

'Damn' impressive, tough boy,' the Box V twister said through gritted teeth. 'Now just hoist your mitts!'

5

'GET OFFA MY GRASS!'

At least two of the fellows closing in on Drift were those he'd already bested once, in Two Springs, and they evidently bore him a grudge for it. He reacted instinctively.

Abruptly abandoning his exhausted demeanour, he grabbed the Box V hand nearest him by an arm, and whirled the man between himself and Feffer's shotgun. A scattergun was menacing, but it wasn't the best weapon when your pards were in range of its devastating blast of undiscriminating pellets.

Feffer hesitated to shoot with the awkward weapon at close quarters for fear of cutting down his comrades with the fan of fire.

As others in the team backed off hurriedly,

Drift hurled the man he'd grabbed at Feffer, violently.

The man slammed into Feffer, who dropped the shotgun. They both went down in a heap. By the time they were picking themselves up, Feffer reaching again for the gun, Drift had drawn the .45 packed in his holster.

'Don't try it!' he barked. 'Or I'll blow you in half. And I'll do it just the same if anyone else makes a move against me.'

Drift could only hope they'd believe his bluff. He wasn't a murderer and there was no way he could intimidate them all for long with just one handgun.

But the issue was resolved for him. Un-noticed in the heat of the fist-fight, two riders had been approaching. The sudden clop of horses' hoofs on the sun-baked ground where the wagon was halted announced the pair's arrival.

They were a burly, reddish-faced man and a pretty young woman aged about twenty. The man wore a black broadcloth suit and a wide white Stetson, with a heavy gold watch-chain across a fancy vest; the girl, a cowboy's collarless shirt, neckerchief and Levis and a wide-brimmed straw hat. They had the same clear blue eyes, but beyond that and a fair-skinned resemblance the likeness stopped. Or did it?

Both sat their saddles with the assurance of the born rider. Drift couldn't remember having seen a girl who looked more at home on the back of a horse.

Was this the big-wheel Box V owner, Kiliaen Van Dam, and his daughter, Rebecca? It had to be, and Zachary Emmett, rising groggily to his feet, confirmed it.

'Howdy, Big Dutch. Hi-ya, Rebecca.'

'Howdy, Zack,' Van Dam said, stiff-backed on his tall horse. 'What the hell is going on here? Ain't you fellers supposed to mending the fence where the goddamned cow-thieves broke it down?'

He seemed not to notice the .45 in Drift's fist, or that a stranger was with his crew.

'We were,' Zack said, 'till this salty young

no-good came ridin' up, askin' for a job. He's a troublemaker!'

The rich cattleman turned a frowning gaze on Drift, like a feudal lord observing, since it was drawn to his attention, that one of the serfs was not his own property. He didn't look the kind of man who'd make concessions, even for a harmless drifter.

Drift glared straight back up at him, though the hot, bright sun and his bruised face told him to squint. He also noticed that Big Dutch's weren't the only pair of blue eyes turned his way. Rebecca Van Dam was curiously looking him up and looking him down. She'd know him if she saw him again.

He wondered what the girl made of his dusty and battered appearance and whether he passed her minute examination. He also had the feeling her thoughts ran along different lines from her grimfaced father's; that she didn't find what the scrutiny told her unwelcome.

Big Dutch boomed, 'Pull your freight, you

young whelp! Didn't you see the sign back over the trail? It's goddamn' big enough, or can't you read?'

'Sure I can read,' Drift said, conscious of a swollen lip that thickened his speech, 'but I was led to believe you had vacancies. I'm pretty good with a rope and don't mind menial chores off-season either. Moreover, I don't like being pushed around by no signs. Nor range bosses who get shucks in their snoots.'

While Big Dutch was giving Drift his marching orders, and Drift was answering back, his daughter was leaning over in her saddle and speaking quietly to Emmett, whose eyes narrowed and brows knitted.

Big Dutch wasn't prepared to listen to Drift's case.

'I've heard enough. Get offa my grass! If I see you around again, you'll be run off, and you won't answer back then, take my word on it!'

Moments later, Van Dam and his daughter rode off, the stern cattleman leaving the overseeing of Drift's removal in the foreman's hands.

It was a measure of Zack Emmett's formidableness that he was already recovered from his dazing clash with Drift. He was a hard man, that was certain.

Coldly, he told Drift, 'All right. I've decided to take a chance. You're hired.'

Drift's bashed ears were still buzzing. 'Do I hear you right, Emmett? Am I getting a job?'

Emmett shrugged. 'Seems like. Thirty dollars a month and feed. I 'preciate tough guys, but don't start any more trouble.' He sounded like an army sergeant laying down the law to a recruit he didn't much like.

'I can usually manage to stay out of trouble,' Drift said mildly. But his brain was awhirl. He stabbed a guess at what, or rather who, had prompted the surprise turnaround. 'Is this Miss Van Dam's idea?'

'Yeah ... waal, 'smatter of fact, it is. Miss Rebecca gets these romantic notions. She's still at a foolish age.'

'She seemed a nice, well set-up girl,' Drift said stoutly.

He remembered her competence with the horse, the oval face with its firm chin, so expressive of strong will, and her unmasked interest. Something about her had told him that once she'd decided on a thing, she'd see it done or know the reason why it wasn't. Maybe in that way she had the character of her unbending father.

Emmett glowered. 'Mebbe, but don't you mess with her, y'unnerstand? She said takin' you on would give me the chance to show a dirty saddle-tramp who's range boss here ... that I could knock the pride outa you.'

Drift wasn't sure he liked the dirty saddle-tramp appellation, or even if those were truly the words she'd said about him, but he knew her father expected him to be thrown off the Box V.

'What about her pa?' he asked. After all, if the owner of the place said there wasn't a job for him, it meant there wasn't, and that should be the end of it.

Emmett laughed cynically. 'Don't you worry 'bout that, kid. She'll square it with her pa. But just remember, her an' me are the only two people Big Dutch'll listen to.'

'Fine. The job is plenty enough for me – it buys me the chance to be close enough to where I want to be.'

'Huh...? What kinda big talk is that? The job buys you nothin' – 'cept grief!'

The fencing crew completed its task and Drift returned with the bunch to the ranch headquarters. He was struck with awe at his first look.

The main building was a big hacienda, porticoed and handsome, set on rising ground with its own private, walled yard shaded by a huge mariposa. Around it were clustered two barns, corrals and several log-built sheds, which Drift took to be stables, a blacksmith shop and the like.

Further away was a long, low bunkhouse with many windows. What appeared to be the cook shack and mess were tacked on the end. A long table inside was flanked by benches that would seat up to thirty men. Ten or so were there now, finishing eating and talking in low tones.

Emmett's quarters, as range boss, were in a compact split-log cabin midway between the bunkhouse and the 'top house'. In one pole corral, a remuda of ponies cantered. The poles were assembled with geometric precision; the animals were first-class young horseflesh, spirited and playful in the sunshine.

In the bunkhouse, Lew Farrer stuck out his hand. 'Let bygones be bygones, eh, Drift? Looks like you're ridin' for the brand after all.'

That night, from the bunkhouse chat and back-chat with his new Box V pards, Drift learned the set-up.

'Sure,' Lew said, in his new role as a fellow who'd do to ride the river with, 'we'll tell yuh how the wind's a-blowin' and the dust's a-flyin'.'

He explained that Zack Emmett was top

dog and could generally do no wrong as far as Big Dutch was concerned. Looser tongues said the cattleman would approve if his daughter were to decide to marry the tough range boss.

This tied in with what Drift had learned in Two Springs from the saloon man, Wes Gruber. Big Dutch apparently owed the one-time gunhawk Zachary Emmett for past services that had been rendered without too much care for legal niceties, but with ruthlessness, efficiency and a degree of circumspection that had left the Van Dam name unsullied.

'If it pans out how Zack wants it,' said Lew's pal Pete, 'one day he'll have full control of all the Van Dam holdings.'

'He marries Miss Rebecca, it'll happen,' Lew agreed. 'Mind you, speakin' plain, I figger the girl's life'd be hell once the old man was out of the picture. Most everyone 'cept Big Dutch knows you don't get along with Zack less'n you're ready to kiss his boots from time to time.'

'Also, that he's fickle where ladies is concerned and has wide tastes in them an' likker both,' Pete added.

'Yep,' Lew said. 'Zack's gone the gaits, an' his ring-tailed tooters on the panther piss would have the likes of us poor cow-waddies snooze-marooed – a-seein' elephants and a-hearing owls.'

Pete nodded sagely. 'He sure is tough as a boot an' twice as high.'

Drift wondered if Rebecca knew these reported shortcomings of her father's foreman. From the interested glances she'd cast Drift's way, he figured she in no way considered herself spoken for.

The startling thought occurred to him that Rebecca didn't like Zachary Emmett and aimed to damage the foreman's good standing with her father by tricking him into hiring a drifter, himself, against Big Dutch's expressed wishes. Suppose she neglected to 'square it with her pa'?

Drift could well believe this possible. The arrogant Zack would surely be blinded to the trap by his number-one ambition – to impress the girl, win her hand and thereby achieve control of the Van Dam empire. Drift figured his own position here was chancy at best, depending very largely on Rebecca's motives and what she decided to say or not say to her father.

'Miss Rebecca now,' he probed his new informants, 'what kind of young lady is she?'

'Five foot two, eyes of blue,' Pete said jokingly.

Lew, more reflective, said, 'I'll take a paralysed oath she ain't stand-offish. She never dresses fit to kill, but jest ranch clothes like yuh saw today, by which she does right. Out here, a gal ain't got no more use for city clothes than a hog has fer a side-saddle. She's her pa's daughter. An' I don't mean by that she does what he tells her, but somep'n else. Big Dutch wants her to have social standing, all the comforts.'

Drift said, 'Maybe she'll have them, when she becomes a ranch wife.'

'Between me and you an' the gate post,

Miss Rebecca mightn't make Zack nor any man a good ranch wife – she sure don't love cookin' or keepin' house. Reckon she'd be tooth an' toenail ag'inst such. She wants to be a boss cattleman her own self!'

'I think I savvy what you mean,' Drift said.

He wasn't reassured by one bit of what he'd learned. Too many folks on the Box V had agendas that boded him no good at all.

And he had a feeling he was riding into an ambush.

6

A DIRTY TRICK

With the days growing along toward winter, Drift expected to be assigned chores that made scant call on cowpunching skills. Accordingly, though he trusted Zack Emmett no more than he'd trust a diamondback rattler, he wasn't overly suspicious when the range boss detailed him next morning to ride to Two Springs to pick up the mail. It was a trail he knew in country so far foreign to him.

'Oh, look here, Garrity,' Emmett growled, when Drift made off to fetch his black, 'it's a touchy subject with me, but when a man has his own horse in an outfit, he starts favourin' it.' He jabbed a thumb, indicating the young ponies in their corral. 'That's a

73

new bunch of horses the ol' man just bought. Choose one of them; they need breakin' in some.'

At the corrals, several hands were saddling up. They greeted Drift guardedly, aware of the ill-feeling between him and Zack Emmett.

They looked him over with critical eyes as he ran his own over the new animals, as fresh and lively as when he'd noticed them on his arrival at the Box V home lot.

Drift was drawn by the attractive colouring of a pinto pony. It was maybe the most frisky and mettlesome, too. But what the hell? If he selected this bronc and it was cantankerous, he could demonstrate his skills and garner some handy respect.

He entered the corral and prepared to rope the pinto, shaking out his loop for the toss. On his approach, the excitable pinto broke away from the small herd.

A good omen, Drift thought. Intelligent. Senses my interest.

Having cut out his desired mount, he

made his cast, judging to a nicety the speed and direction of the pony's circuitous travel.

Drift's body was a troubling mass of bruises from his fight with Emmett, but he defied the stiffness and pain in his right arm to bring the pinto to a halt with a strong, firm jerk.

A slow approach and calming talk got him within range to put up a hand and stroke the long nose.

The pinto danced back, unsure of him, but he was persuaded to accept blanket and saddle. He was not an entirely unbroken animal and was accustomed to the routine. Drift put a narrow boot-toe in the stirrup and got hold of the pommel with both hands. But when he leapt astride, the show began.

On a cold morning nearly all young broncs pitched a little or frog-walked when mounted. This was somewhat more than that. Drift nearly blew his stirrups as the pinto wrinkled his spine and 'swallowed his head', getting it between his knees. As it was, for a moment the onlookers saw daylight between denim and leather before Drift got his ass back in the hull.

Then for several minutes, Drift was borne around the corral. The pinto sun-fished and swapped ends, scattering the other broncs from his dust-raising path.

The Box V hands cheered and clapped, some derisively, and Drift knew he'd been had again. Zack Emmett must have known this would happen.

But even then he didn't realize the full extent of the trick the treacherous range boss was pulling on him. He thought it was merely a case of being given a hard time by a spine-jarring, ass-thumping bucker that doubtless had a reputation among the other hands. At this stage, he didn't know it was more.

It needed all his strength and skill to cling on with knees and legs in the attempt to bring the pinto under control. He coasted on the spurs, not so much as scratching the bronc with them. But he took off his hat and used it to fan, or whip, the spirited animal.

The pinto knew all the stunts instinctively,

it seemed. He showed off many styles of bucking and pitching. Drift was equal to them all – as well as determined not to let the bronc get the better of him.

Eventually, after the horse had run through his repertoire and given Drift a thorough shaking-up, he quieted down.

Aching to his bones, Drift patted the horse's neck. Though feeling anything but pleased, he said, 'Good boy. You ain't gonna give any more trouble, are you?'

He could have done with a wash and a rest, but Drift lifted the iron hoop that latched the corral gate and lit out at an easy lope for Two Springs and the post office. The satisfying thought he had was that no one he left behind could think he was a greenhorn after the impressive display of bronco-busting.

He grinned, guessing Zack Emmett had misjudged his ability. 'By a mile,' he murmured to the breeze. 'By a mile...'

When horse and man returned wearily to

the Box V, the true picture emerged.

A burly figure came storming down to the corrals from the Van Dam house. Big Dutch himself, Drift observed. What went on here? The ranch owner was in a fury.

Hands watched from discreet distances, trying to look like they were going about their work, but some of them were snickering.

Drift felt a dawning alarm. Big Dutch was flourishing a fist and toting a buggy whip in the other.

'Get off that horse, cowboy!' he bellowed. 'No dirty 'puncher rides him. Get off, I say!'

Ordered down, Drift let himself slip from the saddle, silently cursing, warily watching the whip. Big Dutch was banging the stock in agitation against his thigh. Plainly, Drift wasn't supposed to be riding the brown-and-white pony, and he knew he'd been suckered into it by Zack Emmett.

The range boss had offered him the choice of the new horses, gambling on him picking the prettiest and liveliest – and knowing that the pinto was for some reason forbidden.

He felt a sick loathing churning in his stomach but forced a smile.

'Sort of sounds like you're wrought up about something,' he said.

'Wrought up?' Big Dutch ranted. 'Great God almighty! Who wouldn't be wrought up? That's my daughter's new pony you're riding – reserved for her exclusive use.'

So now Drift knew. Having carried out Rebecca's wishes in the matter of his hiring, Emmett had tried to put him in bad with both her and her pa. A pretty slick move, Drift had to admit.

'I was acting on your foreman's orders, Mr Van Dam,' Drift said, without much hope he'd be believed. And he wasn't.

'What kinda tall story is that?' Big Dutch roared. 'Do you take me for an idiot? Zack Emmett would never give such orders. He has my full confidence.'

Through the black mists of his consuming anger, a new thought visibly struck the cattle-man. 'Say, all the hands here know that's my daughter's horse... Ain't you the jasper who was shown off my range yesterday?'

Inwardly Drift groaned anew. Not only had he been double-crossed by Emmett – Rebecca hadn't squared his presence with her pa. Either she'd never said she would and it was Emmett's omission or – as he'd surmised before – she'd neglected to deliberately, maybe in order to undermine her father's faith in the demandingly ambitious range boss.

He was up to his neck in muddy waters here.

Big Dutch cracked the whip at his toes and he jumped back. 'What have you got to say for yourself before I thrash the shirt off your back, mister?'

Drift swallowed hard. He'd once known a man who'd been whipped in Mexico after running foul of the *rurales*. He'd been tied to a post and his punishment had gone on for two hours. His back still carried the scars; at night, he'd had dreams that would wake him up, screaming.

Drift cast his eyes around and saw two minimally hopeful developments. Zack Emmett was swaggering over from his neat cabin, and Rebecca Van Dam had just come through the iron-bound yard gate of the big house and was tripping down the grassy slope.

Maybe they meant to intervene.

Though both were making what looked like an effort to conceal their haste, it seemed a race was on to see who would reach the autocrat and tell his or her story first.

Stalling for time, Drift said, 'I'll rub your daughter's pinto down good. He needs it.'

Big Dutch was fit to explode with apoplexy, but Zack Emmett reached them and cleared his throat to gain attention.

'I knew this bastard was a bad 'un, Big Dutch. Now Miss Rebecca might believe it, too. It was her idea to give him a chance an' take him on. She gets such girlish notions at times.'

Well, Zack had made sure he got his word

in; was keeping his nose clean, Drift thought.

Regardless of the notions Emmett ascribed to her, Drift thought 'girlish' was hardly the word for the fully mature young woman who reached her father, all hot and flustered, as he revolved the whip handle in his right hand in small, ever faster circles, building up to taking a second crack at the man who'd dared to go up against his rule. The lash was rippling.

'No, Pa!' she cried. 'You mustn't beat the poor man. It's none of his fault. It's probably mine. I *did* ask Zack to hire him.'

Big Dutch frowned. 'Then why didn't you mention it, Rebecca?'

The girl's discomfiture increased. 'I guess I – er – I forgot. I didn't think it'd come to anything like this.'

'I don't know, gal,' her father said. 'You can't take a shine to just any han'some young bum that struts along, you know. In your position, it ain't proper or ladylike.'

'Maybe I don't want to be a lady!' Rebecca

retorted gamefully – and scandalously for a maiden of her times. Her eyes met Drift's all at once and she dropped them in confusion.

Again, Drift thought she was a lovely girl, with her glowing cheeks and strands of wispy, honey-gold hair escaping from under her wide-brimmed straw hat. In her blue eyes lurked a defiant passion that issued a challenge to any interested male.

Yesterday, it had been a 'come and get me if you can' expression – lambent, latent, the memory of it had been intensely provoking and had haunted his night's dreams. Today, the hint of contriteness was no less provocative. And what he saw flickering in her eyes before she dropped them filled Drift with wild, impossible hopes.

She was, if Drift had any knowledge of such matters, a veritable explosive charge – waiting for the one man to appear whom she'd dare to let put the flame to the fuse. The incredible question came to Drift's mind: was he that man?

And if he was, what about her father's

alleged choice for her – Zack Emmett?

The time wasn't fitting to ponder such remarkable questions. Big Dutch, having no conception of the more subtle tensions in the air, dragged their thoughts back to the pony.

'But the pinto, Rebecca – this nobody had the brass nerve to help hisself to a hoss – not a dead-head but a prize pony bought for your own use alone!'

'He's a horse-thief,' Emmett said, returning to the chase. 'We oughta string him up.'

Drift protested, 'Why, you lying–! You sent me to the post office in Two Springs yourself.'

'Sure, but I didn't tell you to steal Miss Rebecca's pinto.'

'I've ridden him back, haven't I?' Drift was exasperated.

'After you made him lay his belly in the sand.'

'A young hoss like that needs a good run. I've said – I'll unsaddle him and see he gets all the attention he needs.'

Emmett turned to his employer. 'A two-bit, sham hard man with a smart mouth! He'll likely lift anythin' we don't have roped down is my considered opinion. You was right, Big Dutch – shoulda never've hired the scum on. Why not whip the shit outa him right now?'

'You're right, Zack,' Big Dutch said, and flourished the whip so it whistled. 'He needs to be taught a damn' good lesson.'

But disregarding the danger of catching the rawhide lash herself, Rebecca thrust her way between the two men, small fists clenched.

'Oh, stop it, will you? I said it was my fault he's gotten off on the wrong foot with you, Pa.' Her face suddenly brightened as though something else had just occurred to her. 'What's more, it was me who told him he could take the pinto. I thought the pony could do with the exercise.'

All three men knew she was a liar. But her father wasn't about to take her in hand and call her one – leastways, not in front of hired help. Nor was Zack Emmett, having limited the damage she'd already done him, going to foul his nest one bird dropping further. And Drift, of course, was plain relieved by the reprieve. Moreover, he wanted to stay in this country to resolve the big issues of his life, which meant he needed a base and a job to keep body and soul together.

Pretty Rebecca Van Dam was throwing him a lifeline and just possibly a whole lot more. Who could complain about that?

Big Dutch said gruffly, 'Women! There's no accounting for them. All right, tumble-weed, you stay. But from here on in, you watch your step, and mind you don't take liberties with my daughter, you hear?'

'No, sir!' Drift said.

Zack Emmett looked sick. His dirty trick to dispose of Drift had blown up in his sour face.

But it was only the beginning of the trail. Drift had no illusion he wouldn't try something else, and that he'd be whole lot more leery next time.

7

SWEET TALK, BITTER THOUGHTS

Days followed nights and stretched into a week of tedious off-season chores on the Box V. Drift found little privacy in the bunkhouse, but that he was long used to, in many similar lodgings and on trail-drives. He spent the evenings trying to lessen the boredom of his existence: a little gambling with Lew Feffer and his pards, some reading, and the inevitable telling of tall tales.

When he could, Drift would steer the tale-telling around to earlier times, the district's gold rush, and Highgrade Pocket, the ghost town in the mountains.

But he learned little new, since these men had all come here since Highgrade Pocket had deteriorated to its present status, and the cattle-raising business – and Big Dutch's Box V – had been in the ascendant. What he heard about Mad Dungaree Dan tended to reinforce his conjectures, startling though these were and full of damning implications.

'The old miner's plumb loco,' Lew said adamantly.

'What made him loco?' Drift asked.

'Why, they do say he had this beautiful wife – a Mexican woman of high birth called Consuela who he shamed an' stole away from her fam'ly,' Pete said. 'When she died, it turned his wits somep'n fierce.'

Lew said, 'She anythin' like that M'liss, I c'n unnerstan' it. Wow! Ain't she a hot li'le piece o' goods, eh, Drift?' He laughed and dug him in the ribs. 'We all know that's whys yuh're so in'erested in the Pocket. Yuh wanna git inta her drawers! Waal, you an' me both, brother, an' a whole passel of other fellers. Jest remember – most all of 'em as has tried to grab Mad Dan's beauties have ended up *dead*.'

Drift denied their interpretation of his

interest, but not too insistently.

Only first-hand investigation would firm up a theory he had into fact, and such was not among feasible options for the moment. Getting here had left him on the bones of his ass, and he needed the Box V money and feed to live.

The bright spots in Drift's life at this time were supplied by Rebecca. She seized every chance to come by wherever he might be working. On rest days, she delighted in riding out with him, on the pretext of showing him over the ranch.

'You know this range pretty well, don't you, Rebecca?' Drift commented. The formal 'Miss' had been quickly dropped at her request.

'Of course I do,' Rebecca said. 'I ride a lot, and talking to Pa and the Box V crew has given me a pretty good idea of where our cows graze and so on.'

They checked their horses on the crest of a rise. The sleeves of her man's shirt were rolled up and she waved a sun-browned arm.

'Isn't it all wonderful? I love it so much more than being stuck in the house. Pa thinks I should stay home – keeping his books, writing letters, sending out invitations to his stuffy Cattlegrower's Association gatherings. Not to mention helping with the cooking and doing the sewing.'

'Don't you like those things?'

She wrinkled her nose. 'Not on your life! I'm an outdoors girl.'

'Ever ride up into the mountains?' Drift nodded toward the rising terrain to their west.

'Sometimes. Dad runs Box V stock right up into the foothills. The meadows there are rich with grass, well-watered and green even at times when the flats are sun-scorched.'

'Know anything about the ghost town – about Highgrade Pocket?'

Rebecca eyed him uncertainly for a moment. Then she said, 'The Pocket is a horrible place. Pa hates it, and so do I. It was the best thing ever for this country when the mines played out after five years.

I've heard they attracted undesirables in great number, and they disrupted ranching activities. There were many cases of cattle-rustling and horse-thieving. Men had to be hanged for it.'

'Isn't there still an older miner and his family living up there?' Drift prompted.

'You mean Mad Dungaree Dan and his daughters?'

'They were the folks I had in mind.'

'Forget them!' Rebecca snapped. 'The old man is a murderer, and the two girls not much better, I should think ... like wild animals.'

Drift decided to drop the subject. 'Well then, shall we turn for home?'

'Oh, no, I think not. If we go back, I'll be duty-bound to attend to all those things I don't want to do, and people will watch us and talk. I've brought food along in a saddle-bag for a picnic.'

'Sounds fine to me,' Drift said whole-heartedly.

They put their horses into an easy canter,

heading for where the mountain range lifted a rugged shoulder against the blue sky. Eventually, they came to trees, where they slowed to a walk in the shade between the tall and stately columns of the timber. The pungency of spruce- and pine-like perfume filled their lungs.

Finding a place that was still, cool and restful, they stopped to eat, drink and enjoy one another's company as young people who find a mutual liking will always do.

Drift soon discovered the Box V didn't provide full days of work for the skeleton crew retained for the winter. So much for the claims made by the 'hard-worked' Lew Feffer and his pals. It also became apparent to Drift that even Zack Emmett had time on his hands. Which wasn't a good thing. Emmett hadn't failed to notice the developing friendship between himself and Rebecca.

Naturally, the bitter range boss begrudged it, and though he said nothing, he looked more and more put out.

One day, his actions led Drift to believe he was choosing to express his resentment and deliver a warning in an oblique but frightening way.

'Let me show you somethin', kid,' he said.

'Sure,' Drift said, not knowing what to expect but reluctant to antagonize the man further.

A heap of whiskey bottles had been brought out the back of the bunkhouse in an attempt to tidy up a place that was generally unclean and had a thriving population of lice and bedbugs.

'See them dead soldiers?' Emmett said.

Drift nodded. 'Was about time we did some housework. We ain't been too busy.'

'Toss one across the yard, kid – far as you can.'

Drift picked up a bottle and threw it. Emmett went into a gunfighter's crouch, his hands hovering over the walnut-gripped .45s thonged low on his thighs. The instant the bottle stopped moving, Emmett palmed his right gun and blasted it to smithereens.

He grinned at Drift mirthlessly.

'Still plenty good with a handgun, ain't I?'

Drift agreed again. 'Sure.'

'Now we'll try it left-handed. Throw again,' he ordered.

A second bottle went the way of the first, sharp green chips flying every which way and glinting in the sun.

'Aw, it's too easy,' Emmett crowed. 'Let me show you how I can do it real fast. Throw one in the air.'

Drift hurled the bottle up. Emmett's right gun jerked out of the cut-down holster in a blur, faster than Drift's eye could follow. It flamed, roared. And the bottle shattered in mid-air, coming down to the dusty ground in a shower of splinters.

Emmett dropped the smoking gun back in the holster.

'Kinda scary what a man can do with his guns, ain't it? Anyone riles me bad enough, he's likely to head for Boot Hill so fast he'll never know what hit him.'

'Nice shooting,' Drift said without warmth.

'Be damn' sure you don't ever forget it. When it comes to slingin' a gun, I do it better'n you ever will. For a fact. Of rights, I could carve a dozen notches on these guns. *Twelve.* That's the number I've killed in my time.'

'That's a fair tally.' Drift was properly sober about it. He wasn't dumb and the message was clear. In this outfit, Zack Emmett gave the orders and you did what he said. Or else.

Emmett clapped his strong, hard hands. He brightened his expression.

'Let you an' me be pards, kid. I gotta a lot o' respect for you, an' you're a funny man. We should make our peace. I can help you, see?'

'How's that so?' Drift was baffled by the direction the discussion was taking. But he suspected Emmett was telling him to take less of an interest in Rebecca Van Dam. His next words bore it out.

'You want a woman, right? An' I've heard you been askin' around 'bout the hermit of

Highgrade Pocket. But you're just like every young buck, an' we know what you're really interested in, don't we?'

'We do?'

'Too right we do. I hear you've already had an eyeful of one of them ghost town belles. A real tease an' a temptation. All untasted an' untaught an' a-waitin' up there on the mountain.'

'Frankly, I've not given a thought to the subject,' Drift said, though it was not one hundred per cent true. 'But I would like a scout around in Highgrade Pocket ... a word with Mad Dungaree Dan wouldn't go amiss.'

Emmett laughed cynically, harshly. 'You go up there half-cocked, the only talkin' Mad Dan's apt to do is with his rifle. He's mighty handy with a gun and a knife. Like myself in that regard, you might say.'

'What do I do then, Emmett?'

'You can leave most of it to me. Box V's been losin' cows, just a few head a time, but a damn' nuisance to Big Dutch. Shan't be hard to persuade him – he's been complain-

96

in' considerable. The galoot responsible runs 'em off, smashin' fences and suchlike, as you've seen. He rustles 'em an' butchers 'em is my guess. We got to get Mad Dan accused of it. Could be him anyway. Him an' the gals ain't got much by way of solid vittles up there. Just game an' the stuff the gals grow.'

Drift frowned. 'How does that help?'

'It gives us an excuse to raid Highgrade Pocket in force with Big Dutch's say-so. We'll seize Mad Dan, hand him over to the law in Two Springs, an' the two gals'll be kind of available for all of us boys to do as we will, if you get my meanin'. Won't be no need anymore for you to be a-botherin' Miss Rebecca. You follow?'

Drift sucked in his breath. It was an outrageous proposition, and in one way it could further his own plans, but he felt guilty about what the dirty-minded foreman had in mind for the 'ghost town belles'.

He prevaricated. 'Maybe I'll talk to my bunkhouse pards about this.'

Zack Emmett was undaunted by the

suggestion. 'Go ahead. Way I got it figgered, they'll jump at the chance to lay their hands on those gals. You'll be fightin' to get your share of the fun. Think on it anyways. But not for too long, an' don't forget what I said about stayin' away from the boss's daughter.'

He swung on his heel and stomped off, confident that he'd made his points.

When Drift ran Zack Emmett's ideas past Lew Feffer and company, it disturbed him that they approved of the exploit to a man.

'I'd admire to have a piece o' breakin' in them ghost town gals,' Lew said. ''Course, Zack'll claim first rides hisself, whatever he's promisin' us,' Lew said.

Drift was confused. 'But surely his plan is to get me involved with them, so he'll have a clear run with Rebecca.'

Pete, who was testing his skills throwing a knife at a picture on the bunkhouse wall, scoffed at his naïvety.

'We told yuh 'bout his whiskey drinkin' an' secret tomcattin', didn't we? He visits with cheap, trashy women out to make a fast buck the easiest way they can. His *love* for Miss Rebecca is nine parts love for the ol' man's money an' land. O' course, he don't want no one gettin' too cosy with her, that'd queer his pitch, but havin' Miss Rebecca all lined up won't stop him pokin' them unbroke ghost town gals.'

Drift's concerns were deepened on all fronts. He didn't trust the way Zack Emmett was buddying up to him, accompanied as it was by unspoken threats such as the demonstration of his gunfighting skills.

He was in two minds whether he should co-operate in the conspiracy against Mad Dungaree Dan. He might well have a score of his own to settle with the old recluse, yet was this the way to do it?

In Zack Emmett, Drift saw the personification of his own dark side – the domineering, immoral range boss was the person he could easily be akin to if he went along with this adventure in what amounted to outlawry.

8

PLANTING EVIDENCE

Two days later, Zack Emmett came to Drift with what he said was an unexpected snag.

'The ol' man wants evidence, he says. He won't have us stirrin' up the Two Springs law an' all – leastways, not without we got us a good case that Mad Dungaree Dan has been rustlin' Box V stock.'

Drift was not displeased. He hadn't resolved the dilemma he was in over the whole deal.

He couldn't see Mad Dungaree Dan surrendering meekly to an unofficial posse of aggressive and randy cowhands. Shots would probably be fired. What if Zack Emmett put Drift in the forefront of the attack, and Mad Dan shot him dead? Or come to think about it, what if he could be made to stray 'accidentally' under friendly, Box V fire? A skilfully placed bullet in the back. Either of those circumstances would serve Emmett's number-one purpose as well as any other. And Emmett's purpose, of course, was to remove Drift's pesky competition for Rebecca.

Relieved, Drift said, 'So it's all off then?'

'Bet your sweet life it ain't!' Emmett said. 'We just get a little more sly is all.'

'How so?'

'Why, we start off by makin' sure we do get the evidence.' He smiled in grim self-satisfaction. 'Ain't nothin' Zack Emmett can't do around here if he puts his mind to it.'

Drift was at a loss to know exactly what Emmett meant, but he made himself grin. 'I guess you've got a plan.'

'I certain-sure have, kid. Listen close, because you're the man I can trust to do it right. Kinda smart an' with plenty of guts.'

'You reckon? What does it involve?'

'You'll drive a buckboard up there with a stack of Box V-branded cowhides, a spade and some sacks of quick-lime. You'll bury the hides in a gully back of Mad Dan's place in the Pocket, tipping the lime over them. Later, when the law digs 'em up, they'll take it as evidence of Mad Dan's guilt and his bid to destroy it.'

'Hmm,' Drift muttered, appalled by the sneakiness of it. 'Mean, but I guess it'll work a treat.'

'Sure as shootin' it will. You just do it real good an' be sure to watch your step, kid.'

'You don't have to tell me that. Were Mad Dan to catch me up there with the hides and the lime, the fat'd be truly in the fire.'

Later, when Drift confessed the same worries about Emmett's scheme to Lew Feffer, the hand replied, 'I shouldn't worry 'bout that partic'lar. If'n Mad Dan sees yuh, he's gonna shoot first without askin' questions anyways.'

Naturally, Drift wasn't reassured, but he knew he had to do what he was told. The only alternative he might be given to following Emmett's wishes would be to pull his freight.

He was to head out for the ghost town before first light – before the Box V, and hopefully Mad Dungaree Dan and his daughters, began their day.

Zack Emmett was on hand when the time came to see him off, and he pointed to the foothills.

'You head west for the broken country, goin' through the timber. Then an escarpment of red rock'll force you to veer north. It ain't much of a trail for driving a buckboard till it strikes the old stage road to Highgrade Pocket. The road's a mite better then, though nowadays it's full of holes an' precarious. The goin' gets kind of wild – but it threads through the notches in the ridges and round the worst of the upthrusts. Just use your head an' take it steady, kid. You'll do fine...'

An hour later found Drift in some of the most rugged terrain he'd known. On the rim of a steep bluff, where the road was just wide enough for the buckboard's safety, he pulled up to allow his two horses a breather.

He found himself looking back over a giant's maze of rock – a haphazard assembly of massive cliffs, narrow gulches, winding canyons and crumbling pinnacles. Ahead towered more peaks, the slopes splotched with dark, shadowy timber that masked the jagged granite.

The road, as Emmett had promised, was hardly fit for a wheeled vehicle. And as yet, there was no sight of the ruins of Highgrade Pocket. The final miles of road, concealed by forest growth and the hairpin turns, could be worse.

Just what had Drift let himself in for?

Wilderness was reclaiming the plundered lands around what was left of Highgrade Pocket. Each year, as Melissa moved inexorably toward her own maturity and the un-accustomed problems that came with it, so did the regenerating forest and the mining-gouged mountainside forever challenge her curiosity, bringing perils other than of the two-legged variety her pa was so adept at deterring.

She couldn't read books but she could read sign, knew how to trap and was learning to shoot – when Pa would let her borrow one of his guns, that was. Her trophies included the pelts of ermine, marten and squirrel. She could also spear rainbow trout with a sharpened stick, which was no mean feat since when you thrust you had to make fine allowances for the distorting effects of the water.

There were no flies on Melissa. But she aspired to be a grower as well as a hunter and gatherer, and was cultivating a small patch of corn. To her consternation, a bear took a liking to the succulent crop.

'Look, Issy,' she told her sister. 'The paw marks say bear.' She pointed to the soft, churned-up soil. 'Fool thing! It rip out more maize plants than it ate. All spoiled. Chewed up.'

The grave-faced Isabella shrugged. 'No help for it, M'liss. It's the way things are. All the people are gone from here, except us. We must put up with whatever happens.'

Melissa went to her father and though he grumbled, he rustled up a bear trap. It had been stashed away among the mouldering junk left in the remains of the Highgrade Pocket hardware store, a frame structure originally thrown up with less thought to its own permanence than to that of the goods it stocked.

The trap was chained that night to a heavy deadfall marking the perimeter one side of the corn bed, yet in the morning it was gone. Amidst fresh destruction, the snapped-off end of the rusty chain was still attached to the tumbled tree. Bushes round about were flattened to the earth. But there were no trap, no bear to be shot.

The track of the bear and the trailing trap was well defined.

'Give me gun and I follow,' Melissa said.

Mad Dungaree Dan tamped down the

tobacco in a large and blackened corncob pipe with slow deliberation and shook his grizzled head.

'No yuh don't, child. Tha's an ol' beast – mebbe lazy, but big an' hungry. Likewise, evil-tempered with a trap clamped on his hind laig.'

Melissa knew better than to defy her father openly, but she determined to kill the bear and retrieve the trap it had dragged away.

She had an idea the silly beast would come back that night to gobble more of the corn, injured though it was. When it came close enough, she'd put a bullet in its head. Pa would surely forgive her for taking his gun when she gave him back the lost trap.

Accordingly, when a long day was at last over and Mad Dan retired to the bed he shared with her elder sister – and she knew he was sated with the comforts he took from her and could hear his heavy, rhythmic breathing – she helped herself to his Yellow-boy carbine and crept stealthily from the house.

Wrapped in a blanket, she stationed herself behind a heap of weed-grown spoil overlooking her bear-ravaged corn patch. The smashed rocks and dirt she crouched among were a mournful monument to long-past endeavours when men had flocked here after the discovery of the lode that had brought Highgrade Pocket into being.

Keeping vigil from this dreary spot proved not as easy as she'd thought it would be. Unwittingly, she dozed off.

Along about dawn, she awoke to peer over the rocks – and to find the bear had arrived while she slept.

It sat on its haunches in the corn patch some fifty yards away, the cruel trap still attached to its bloodied hind leg. It was black in colour and in its misery.

The old brute was evidently in great pain, shaking its shaggy head aimlessly and taking the odd, ineffectual swipe at the instrument that caused it.

Melissa felt pity in her heart. She'd end its plight swiftly. She raised the carbine to her shoulder and sighted on the spot midway between the bear's eyes.

But her relative inexperience with the powerful firearm, her haste in her freshly woken state, and her excitement all combined against her. When she jerked instead of squeezed the trigger, the carbine's brass butt plate kicked against her shoulder, and the muzzle lifted.

Even then, it didn't seem to matter. A tuft of black fur flew as the bullet glanced off the top of the bear's scalp. The huge beast toppled with a ground-shaking thud.

Melissa's spirits leaped at her easy triumph. Now all she had to do was unlock the trap from the bear's damaged leg and hump it back to her pa as the prize and proof of her capabilities.

She'd put the carbine down and was rushing to act on these intentions when the 'dead' bear rolled and lumbered to its feet, blinking bloodshot eyes. It saw Melissa running toward it. Spittle drooled from its mouth and it gave a terrifying roar of agony and anger.

Her shot had merely grooved its thick skull, momentarily stunning it. Now it was up – 400 pounds of hunger, pain and vengeful wrath.

Drift Garrity's pair toiled up one more gradient, the buckboard's iron-tyred wheels crunching on the rubble of the old roadway. Then the huddled shapes that could only be Highgrade Pocket loomed into view. Behind, lemon light in the eastern sky was steadily brightening; ahead, a spectral white moon was still visible in the west, sinking fast toward the jagged skyline beyond the ruined town.

Drift glimpsed weather-beaten buildings aged by sun and wind, few of them whole or standing completely vertical. There were no signs of life. Window glass still intact and reflecting the weak light of the dawning day had the grey and cobwebbed emptiness of dead eyes. But Drift had the eerie and unreasonable feeling he was watched.

111

When a fat rat scurried across the road in front of him, he knew it was time to detour. He steered the horses off the regular road on to ancient wheel traces that had the look of a cutoff. The buckboard, laden with cowhides and sacked quick-lime, lurched and tipped.

The cutoff curved behind a huge and barren heap of blasted rock, plainly carted here and dumped by the former population of goldseekers. Though the way was more bone-jarring here than ever, it placed Drift comfortably out of the ghost town's view. And he'd come far enough and near enough.

He halted the tired horses, got down and began dragging the Box V hides off the buckboard. He'd finished that and was hauling off the sacks of lime when a single shot rang out. Somewhere very close.

He dropped the sack immediately. It burst at his feet, and he whirled about, drawing his Colt revolver, eyes peeled for danger.

Nothing happened for several moments.

Disconcerted though he was by the gun-shot, he was about to carry on with burying the hides. Maybe Mad Dungaree Dan was out hunting; maybe someone else had dared to come up here to do the same. Best to get the job done and clear out, *pronto*.

Then the desolation was shattered a second time by an animal roar. It was succeeded by a high, feminine scream and the mountain hermit's daughter, Melissa, hurtled into sight around the far end of the rock pile.

Behind her came an even more astonishing sight – a full-grown black bear, dragging a length of broken chain and an iron trap with the teeth embedded in its right hind leg.

Unencumbered, a provoked black bear could move at thirty miles an hour. This one, despite the painful handicap of the trap, was loping along fast enough to catch up with the fleet-footed Melissa.

When the girl saw Drift and the buckboard, she broke her pace in surprise, hovering uncertainly for precious split-seconds while she clearly debated with herself whether his unexpected presence called for her to change the direction of her panicky flight.

The bear, great head weaving from side to side on its elongated neck, bellowed again horribly and gathered itself up for a final lunge.

9

DRIFT'S FLIGHT

The bear's canine teeth looked three inches long, its vicious eyes blazed red, and wicked claws armed its mighty paws.

The wild mountain girl was a heartbeat and scant feet away from an horrific death.

Drift's horses shied and backstepped, making the braked buckboard judder and slew across the rough track. For Drift, anxious that his presence in Highgrade Pocket should go undiscovered, the situation couldn't have been worse.

But he didn't have time to think about any of this. Without hesitation, he sprang forward, clear of his nervous horses and the slant-wise buckboard. He raised his drawn .45. He steadied it with both hands. And he promptly fired.

The bullet crashed through the bear's skull, bursting the great brute's brains out through the hole it made on exit and splattering the gore widely. An instant kill. The bear's carcass rose high on its hind legs and toppled backwards, to become an enormous, inert heap of fur and meat.

Melissa came to a stop, raising her hands to her ashen cheeks, staring at the fallen bear. Drift walked uncertainly toward her, a faint smile on his face.

'Looks like I've saved your pretty hide again,' he said. 'I hope you're more appreciative this time.'

The girl peered up at him, 'It *is* you. The nice *hombre* from Two Springs. Today, I thank you. How did you know you must be here to save my life?'

Drift was taken aback. 'I didn't.'

'You married?'

'Am I married?' Drift laughed at the unexpectedness and sharpness of her question. 'Why do you ask?'

'I think you come courting me.'

Drift didn't laugh this time. Whatever had put such a strange idea in the girl's head? He knew it wasn't a question she'd be able to answer. Everywhere, young females her age were liable to form strange notions and fancies. Kept in isolation from normal folks, hers were likely to be stranger than most.

'Nope,' he said firmly. 'I did not.'

Her eyes filled with tears for a moment. 'Then you must be very stupid coming up here for no good reason. Or maybe you are awful brave. Pa will say boys and men come here only to rape Issy or me.'

'He tells you wrong, young lady. I savvy your pa's dead set against all young fellers, but the mountains don't belong to him. Nor even does Highgrade Pocket, or your own self, in fact.'

'No matter!' she cried fiercely. 'He won't let you stay here. He run you off, shoot you – kill you!'

'Nope. I won't let him.'

'He won't kill you? Likely he will, if he

think he no can get rid of you other way.'

Drift dearly wanted to talk more with the unconventional girl; to cross-examine her. To find out all she knew about her father and his strangeness. But he also knew that now he'd been discovered, he had to be out of here, fast.

Emmett's plans had been dashed by a bear and a girl! Just as he'd heard Melissa's shot, so it would have been heard in the town, by her pa and sister. His own shot would have been heard, too.

No sooner had these alarming thoughts taken full hold, backed by Melissa's predictions as to his fate, than Mad Dungaree Dan appeared above them, close to the peak of the crude pyramid of mining debris.

The old-timer spotted them and gave a harsh shout. 'By God! Yuh touch that gal, boy, an' I'll surely cripple yuh with a bullet!'

With the hides and the sacks of lime lying about, it was no time for Drift to stand his ground and argue about his intentions toward the man's nubile daughter. He'd need more luck than a pixie gave a Cornish miner to win the one argument; he'd have no chance of explaining his way out of the other.

The terrain couldn't be worse for making a quick getaway, but he knew the instant he heard the incensed voice of Mad Dan that he had to make a try at getting himself out of there. He leaped aboard the buckboard, let off the brake and lashed the startled horses into motion.

A gun blasted behind him. The slug burned his side, but he was on his way.

Two more shots rang out. Drift thought one lodged in the back of the buckboard. The other spanged off rock someplace alongside and slightly ahead. They ran through a pattering hail of flying fragments, and some of them stung the terrified horses, goading them into a wilder frenzy.

Drift drove hell-for-leather, knowing that once Mad Dan saw the incriminating cowhides and the lime the game would be up; his goose cooked.

Escape or die!

The horses were panicked by the shooting, the whip and the urgent cries of their driver. The unladen buckboard fairly flew, its wheels seemingly making only sporadic, thumping contact with the ground.

Drift wondered if the rig would stand up to the punishment or disintegrate under him. But he couldn't afford to let up. If Mad Dan were to saddle a horse and press the chase, his own animals, drawing a buckboard, would need every minute of their head-start.

Rejoining the old stage road didn't make travel any less an ordeal. The pavement was in bad repair after years of neglect. And added to the irregularities of its surface were switchbacks and hairpin turns, more perilous by far in speedy descent than they'd been in the unavoidably slow ascent.

Wheels span over hundred-foot drops on the one side, while on the other, the body of the buckboard scraped against overhanging walls of granite, the ironwork striking sparks.

The ride devolved into a series of heart-lurching scares for Drift.

But at last, congratulating himself on being away free without a disastrous capsize, he came to the verge of calming and slowing his snorting, head-tossing, slobbering team.

'The loco old man ain't going to catch up now. No ways!' he told the wind.

But unexpectedly, something whipped through the air past Drift's head. A micro-second later, he heard the crashing sound of a carbine and the meaty smack of a bullet entering horseflesh.

His offside horse gave vent to a shrill, nightmarish scream. Its legs collapsed uselessly under it, and it slumped in the traces against its partner.

Shocked, Drift swiftly scanned his surroundings for the source of the evil blow to his rising hopes. And above him he was astonished to see a gaunt, slightly bow-legged figure in faded denim bib-overalls, skylined high on an overlooking bluff.

Mad Dungaree Dan, on foot, had cunningly cut across the mountainside that was his backyard. He'd had no need to follow Drift by the winding road. He'd gotten ahead and drawn a bead on his quarry from the high vantage point.

All this was apparent to Drift in a flash, but he'd no time to curse himself for the fool he'd been not to have foreseen such a manoeuvre.

The stage road at this point was built on a rocky ledge, partly blasted into the steep mountainside. To Drift's right, the ground fell away into a steep and brushy ravine, many hundreds of feet deep.

The surviving horse – encumbered by a dead companion, propelled forward by downhill momentum and the following buckboard – all at once veered and found forelegs and hoofs working on nothing but air.

The last of the roadway rushed out from under the entire assemblage of dead and alive animals, conveyance and man. It became airborne.

Drift was pitched from the buckboard's seat in an involuntary somersault as it tilted from horizontal to perpendicular. The horses and pieces of their tackle whirled in a blur beneath him. The plunging buckboard, coming fast on his heels, struck an outcrop and broke apart into large pieces that surrounded and buffeted him in his fall.

Then trees, bushes and rocks were spinning up in a rush to meet him. He felt a terrible blow to the head. His right shoulder and hip were dashed bruisingly against rocks, but still he fell. Spiky bushes clawed and tore at his clothing.

When he slammed to a standstill, all sense, strength and breath were knocked out of him by the impact. Darkness flooded his brain. Stunned into immobility, he didn't know how a considerable portion of the buckboard's framework fell across his left leg.

He knew no pain. He knew nothing.

Awareness seeped back into Drift's brain.

Light was out there beyond his closed eyelids. But he knew that to open them to daylight would be to open himself to a new intensity of the spasms of pain racking him from a throbbingly bruised temple to a leg that felt like it was gripped in a vice.

He heard a trickle of falling rock. Was that the scree somewhere upslope from him sliding under a man's boot?

Drift kept quite still. Though partly in a stupor, fighting waves of darkness that fogged his returning mental processes, instinct alone was enough to foster caution. A hundred points of sensation, ranging from discomfort to torture, demanded the ease that movement might bring if it were possible. But he kept his eyes shut, his limbs and trunk immobile.

The effort brought a reward, of sorts.

He heard a cackling laugh. Instantly, he placed it: Mad Dungaree Dan.

The old man came closer but his shuffling steps eventually drew to a stop. Possibly the footing was too precarious for him to venture closer. He muttered to himself harshly like the demented person he was reputed and had shown himself to be.

'Ain't gonna risk m' neck to look closer at the good-fer-nothin'. Prob'ly nothin' on him worth a-havin' anyways. Let the buzzards pick the bastard over.'

More dislodged rock skittered down around Drift's motionless form as Mad Dan presumably turned back, continuing his grim soliloquy as he went.

'Wanted to fool aroun' with M'liss, did he? Waal, I told him he'd make number five.'

Drift took it from this that he hadn't yet had the time to see the Box V-branded cowhides and the quick-lime. Surely, once he'd observed them, he would recognize the possibility that his visit to Highgrade Pocket had deeper and more threatening significance.

But for the moment he could take satisfaction that the oldster hadn't seen fit to put a bullet through his brain, and thus make absolutely certain he was left in no shape to interfere with his precious daughters or himself. Maybe he was low on ammo. He'd sure wasted plenty when he'd lit his spectacular shuck from Two Springs.

Drift kept right on feigning death – he felt like it, too – till the sounds of Mad Dan's scrambling retreat had long faded to nothingness amidst the agony in his ringing head. Congratulations on the fooling of Mad Dan weren't in order, however.

The old-timer, Drift found, might still have done for him. When he finally forced himself to open his eyes, he saw the scale of the plight he was in. The largest and heaviest portion of the buckboard's wreckage had fallen across his left leg, effectively trapping it and him. Maybe the leg was broken, though he thought he could still detect feeling in his toes through his myriad pains.

He struggled to wrench himself free. The only result was to cause himself yet greater pain. The blackness surged anew. It came close to swamping his regained senses.

He paused and reconsidered his predicament.

Below him, the ravine bottomed in a bushy stream bed. Above him, the road clung to a narrow ledge halfway down from the high rim. Overhead, the sky had brightened to a brilliant blue. The sun must soon be striking into the depths of the ravine. Caught as he was, Drift couldn't reach the water, and climbing back to the road was going to be a sheer impossibility.

He'd gotten his tail in a crack, and no mistake.

In the growing heat, swarms of black flies were already buzzing with obscene persistence around the broken carcasses of his two horses.

As the sun rose higher, Drift was forced to accept that without help he wasn't going to get out of his plight alive. He wondered what the chances were of Zack Emmett sending out a search party when he failed to return.

Mighty slim, he decided. The range boss might consider his goals sufficiently met by a mysterious disappearance. 'Just another no-good grub-line rider who quit without givin' his notice... Nothing for folks to get het up about.' Once Drift was out of the way, for whatever reason, Emmett would have a clear field with Rebecca and could resume his scheming advances.

As for the rest of the Box V outfit, Drift's friends there were of a fair-weather type. Cowed by Emmett, they could not be relied upon.

The sun made its entrance to Drift's hell. The dazzling orb threw down on him the full intensity of its light and heat. Deliberately, he made himself abandon thinking of the wider issues. His priority became to shift whatever part of him he could into the shade of the broken buckboard and the tangled scrub about him.

But the dappled patchiness of this within his critically confined area of movement was insufficient to protect him in his weakened condition. The scorching rays sapped the last of his strength.

The waves of blackness washed over him

once more, bringing blessed respite from the agony in his body and his head. He felt himself going under like a drowning man.

And then all his senses were lost in a coma...

10

MOUNTAIN ANGELS

Time passed. Nothing moved in the sun-trap of the deep ravine. The next thing Drift was aware of was a damp cloth wiping his face; what felt like the neck of a canteen pressed to his lips.

His eyes blinked open. The angel of mercy was the wild girl, Melissa. She didn't fit the normal image of angels, who were apt to be pictured as fair and serene. But the cool water she brought him was a godsend indeed.

'Drink it slow,' she said. 'Or it do no good and you suffer more.'

'Your pa shot me,' Drift croaked. 'Where is he? Why are you doing this?'

He remembered now how he'd already

been given a sample of her twisted thinking. How did she see him, he wondered? As a foolhardy hero who rescued her from incredible scrapes, like lecherous storekeepers and maddened bears? As another dirty-minded cowhand – an enemy of her father?

More importantly, how could she get him out of this life-or-death fix?

Under his scrutiny, she brushed the long dark hair off her face and over her shoulder. 'Pa not know I come here. He think you dead. I help, or you will die. You take bullet?'

'No, he hit a horse, and now I can't move because of the damn' buckboard across my leg, is all.'

Her dark eyes widened mockingly. 'Is all! You think I can move buckboard and you walk away from here?'

He decided her face was very pretty, but that she was fooling with him and he didn't too much like the way she smelled – of animals and earth.

'No ... no!' he said. 'You gotta go down the mountain to the Box V. Today. Ask to see

Miss Rebecca Van Dam. Get her to send men.'

Melissa shook her head, becoming grave. 'I no can do these things. Pa not let me go. And flatland men not let mountain girl see their fine ladies, not listen to her. She have to run back. Else, they rape her.'

Drift was exasperated. 'That's stupid.'

'Pa say!' she rejoined defiantly. 'I seen it! They attack my sister, Issy. Storekeeper Jennings try it on me.'

'But you'll have to go. There's nobody else.'

'I lift ol' buckboard if I have a little help. I fetch Issy when Pa have his *siesta*. I make her pitch in.'

Drift had his doubts whether the two girls could do the job required, but the offer was better than nothing.

'All right. This afternoon then, but no later, mind. I gotta get outa here or I'm going to fry.'

She looked at him sympathetically. He must have looked a fright with the sweat running down his reddened face although she'd already wiped it more than once.

'I rig up my coat to give more shade,' she said abruptly.

Suiting action to words, she shrugged out of the fringed doeskin coat that with its matching skirt seemed to be her habitual attire. Underneath, she wore no more than a thin *camisa* of Spanish design. Its embroidery had lost its colour and the fabric itself was yellowy-grey with age, but Drift's attention focused itself involuntarily on the pertness of the breasts it covered and the outlines of the nipples that pushed their outlines against its thinness. Just for a moment he thought maybe he wasn't so badly hurt after all.

The girl noticed his gaze.

'You see, I have pretty things from old trunk that was my mother's. I not wholly a savage,' she said, only partly appreciating what stimulated his interest in her state of semi-undress.

Well, Drift thought, the garment probably had been daintily pretty in its day. 'Guess not,' he grunted out of politeness.

She stood over him, propping the coat over a broken piece of buckboard siding so it would shield him from the cruel sun.

Drift was intensely conscious of the closeness to his face of her slim brown legs and, again, the odd muskiness of her scent. He decided this wasn't so bad after all. It wasn't an unclean or sour smell, like some body odours he'd known in his wandering life – just strange.

The coat arranged to her satisfaction, she stepped back.

'I be back later,' she said.

And suddenly, nimbly, she was gone, leaping from rock to rock, heading through the brush that lined the ravine's depths rather than ascending the steep, unsafe slope to the old stage road.

Melissa had left the half-full canteen of water with Drift, and he used it sparingly and gratefully. He ignored the stab of pain each time he tried to wrench his left leg from under the buckboard, but eventually he abandoned any effort to free himself. He could do more damage than good. Better to wait with what patience he could muster for the return of Melissa with her sister. On the positive side, his other aches and the woolliness in his head subsided somewhat.

From the high position of the sun and the length of the shadows, Drift judged it was around one hour after noon when Melissa came back with her sister.

Isabella was no less stunning a young woman than the younger girl, but the North American side of her ancestry was more apparent.

She wore backwoods clothing similar to Melissa's, but it was in better repair, as though she'd subjected it to less rugged use. Or possibly it looked better because Melissa might be wearing the older stuff that was her hand-me-downs. She also wore an air of solemnity that bordered on resignation. Her face was beautiful, but she wasn't at peace – now, or maybe ever.

That her approach to their exploit differed was apparent immediately. She was nervous when Melissa offered Drift some strips of jerked meat and a tin cup of cold beans and tomato which she'd brought along out of a mistaken notion he'd be hungry.

'You said we must free the man so he would go,' she said. A troubled frown creased the smoothness of her brow. 'To offer him sustenance is further defiance of Pa's wishes.'

'Don't fret yourself,' Drift said. 'I'm not hungry anyhow. Just help me get loose from here, will you?'

It was then that Melissa, whose behaviour had shown dumbness about many matters, impressed him with her skills. Besides the food, she'd come equipped with a coiled rawhide lariat. From where had it been stolen, he asked himself uncharitably?

'What do you aim to do with that?'

'I show,' she said simply.

Trailing the rope, she climbed with goat-like agility up the steep slope above the wreckage of the buckboard to where a substantial boulder was firmly embedded. She tossed the end of the rope around the smooth boulder and clambered back down, bringing the rope end with her.

'Now we tie to buckboard and haul on other end of rope. It easier, I think, than we put small hands under buckboard and try to heave off leg.'

Drift saw the sense in the arrangement even before she'd finished her explanation. Though unschooled, Melissa had a clever mind in her pretty head. Moreover, being strong of shoulder as a roper of cattle, he could add his own effort to the operation.

It took three tries before they had the girls' weight and his own muscle properly aligned and co-ordinated to exert maximum lift on the pinning weight of the buckboard. Finally, as it creaked and rose the necessary scant inches off his leg, Drift hurriedly dragged himself free.

The straining girls let go of the rope the moment he was clear. The buckboard crashed back into the dirt, raising dust.

Melissa and Isabella were breathless from their exertions. And Drift realized his problems were far from over.

His leg and foot were badly swollen and when he tried to stand, he promptly fell down again. The leg was incapable of taking his weight. It was either broken or severely bruised – he hoped the latter. But whichever it was, he wasn't going to walk out of the mountains today, the next day, or possibly even the next week.

'I can't use this leg. It's smashed up bad. You'll have to go for other help. Maybe it'll help you at the same time, to get offa this mountain and start a normal life like other girls.'

Melissa was beside herself with fury or disappointment.

'No, no, no!' she cried. 'It not possible, I tell you!'

Isabella accepted the less than satisfactory outcome of their endeavours with what Drift could think of only as a submission to the inevitable.

'We will have to tell Pa, M'liss,' she said in a monotone.

Melissa turned on her. 'You more crushed than nice boy's leg! People right, Issy. You soft-brain. Pa hear what we do, he shoot boy, whip me, whip you. Afterward, he poke you, too, in way natural father shouldn't. I watch animals, birds. They don't do that thing with offspring. He maybe want to poke me, but I never let him. Will cut off his balls, kill myself, before he does!'

Isabella cringed from her, her beautiful face white.

Drift, despite the alarmingly incapacitating pain in his injured leg, was totally shocked by what he thought he was hearing.

'Hey! This won't do. I've gotta get off the mountain somehow. You two are my only hope.'

'You own hope,' Melissa said. 'Leg must mend. Then you walk out.'

'Goddamnit, M'liss! It ain't safe here. I could die before I can make it back to the Box V.'

Melissa looked around, making a quick survey of the ravine. She was very decisive. She pointed to a patch of green, close to the stream. On a south-facing slope, the bigger growth was typical mixed pine, scrub oak and mountain mahogany augmented with broad-leaved scrub in dense clumps.

'We carry you there, mister. I make you hide – shelter – put splints on your leg. Bring you chow, water, every day till leg take weight.'

Drift thought it might be preferable if the girls were to fetch transport – say, Mad Dan's buckboard – and abscond with him to Two Springs. Especially given what M'liss had had to say about the old man's treatment of them. But that had to be longer term. He didn't think he was up to the task of persuading the abused and resigned Issy or the spirited M'liss ... yet.

So he agreed. Putting an arm round each of their shoulders for support, he hopped down to the place Melissa had indicated.

Melissa constructed the hide with the skill

of an experienced woodsman, and in sur-
prisingly little time.

She chose a pine sapling and trimmed it
where it stood before bending over the soft
green wood, pegging it to the earth at the
tip. This was to be the shelter's main frame.
To it, she fixed other branches to make sides
and a roof.

At her suggestion, Isabella collected reeds
from the stream's edge. She weaved these
into a thatch that made as snug a shelter as
Drift could wish. Amazingly, she needed no
tools to accomplish the work except a knife
she carried in the top of her skirt.

The girls manoeuvred Drift into the hide
and placed him on a bed of the leftover
rushes. Melissa fetched a rock from the
stream bed and propped his injured leg on
it.

'I don't think the bone's busted,' Drift
said. 'It's just bruised real bad and bleeding
inside into the muscle.'

Melissa said, 'No matter. You cripple for
now. I strap it.' She fetched two smaller

pieces of the buckboard wreck, carefully selected for size, and tied them as splints to the leg with strips of hide.

Her lean brown hands, Drift noted, were strong and as quick and nimble as the rest of her. He'd never met a girl like her.

But when they left, with Melissa promising to bring blankets, he was far from happy with the arrangements they'd made for him.

What if Mad Dungaree Dan should find him? What if his leg failed to heal? How long would that take anyway? What if some misfortune should prevent the girls from supplying him with the food he'd need? And no one from the Box V was likely to find him hidden here, even if they were to come.

Beyond all that, he was no closer to, and in no fit state to do the job that had brought him into this country.

11

STOLEN INNOCENCE, ALLOTTED GUILT

Two days passed without untoward incident, despite Drift's continuing fears. Largely immobile, he had to content himself with scanning the sky above, watching gathering rains clouds scud over the rocky rim of his prison, and being glad he was alive.

At nights, he heard the howling of coyotes in more distant reaches of the wilderness, the occasional sudden screech of a small animal caught by a hunting mountain cat. In some ways it was preferable to the snoring of fellow bunkhouse inmates, and the fresh air was healthier no doubt.

Melissa had been as good as her word and supplied him with the necessaries of life.

Isabella he hadn't seen again. He worried about that. Her sullen negativity was, on recall, deeply disturbing. The attitude that failure was an inevitability was one that had always frightened Drift.

He broached again the subject of the girls' breaking away from their father's abusive oppression. What they had with the old man was not a life; just a wretched existence.

Melissa was more restrained in her reply this time.

'No – mountain our home. All other place here more terrible than Pa. Maybe one day we go to Mama's home in Old Mexico. She long dead. It very sad. I remember her little. Issy know more. But she afraid. It far way to go to Mexico.'

It was true that Melissa, with her awkward speech and simple directness, struck him as being more at home in the woods and the wild country than in a town like Two Springs.

The Mexican angle was intriguing though. With gentle prompting, Drift was able to piece together from Melissa her family history as far as she knew it.

The girls' mother had been the beautiful Señorita Consuela Cavara and her ancestors were pure Spaniards with no Indian blood in them and spoke nothing but fine Castilian Spanish. Consuela's father, Don Raul, had been proud of his *hidalgo* origins.

A Cavara, it was said, had come out from Old Spain with Hernando Cortez. He was richly rewarded like the rest of the *conquistadores* and founded a great estate.

For more than three centuries the Cavara family were the best of grandees – building churches, feeding the hungry in times of famine by distributing largesse out of their big granaries. They covered the hills with their flocks and herds, created and owned whole villages, as it had been in past ages in the old land.

Eventually, however, in the time of some revolutionary struggle, the *peons* rose up against their good but feudally minded masters. Consuela was kidnapped from La

Casa Cavara during the hostilities and fell into the hands of Luis Velarde, a brutish bandit chieftain sometimes called 'Loco Louey'.

Velarde and his gang were opportunists who had no interest in politics, but indiscriminately rustled stock, robbed banks, stuck up stagecoaches and killed honest lawmen on both sides of the Rio.

Velarde's hideout was in a canyon in poor country off the higher back trails where few men travelled. The place was a fertile oasis amidst barren, wind-scoured desolation. The one sound structure was a long, steep-roofed, stone-walled *posada*, with hitch racks out front. This was Loco Louey's own private dwelling, from where he ruled an empire of crime that straddled the Border and took in, besides general thievery, the cultivation, manufacture and trafficking of narcotics and the 'protection' of *perdidas* – the lost ones – toiling in small-town brothels.

Here, after buying Consuela from the rebel *peons* with much stolen gold, Loco Louey personally deflowered the beautiful *señorita*.

Consuela was devastated. Shamed, she could never return to her proud, noble family should she be so lucky as to escape the bandit community.

But help was unexpectedly at hand in the shape of a wandering *gringo* prospector – Dungaree Dan, then much younger and not quite so mad.

Negotiating a rocky pass in the jumbled country, Dungaree Dan came upon Velarde's hideaway suddenly and quite by chance, as was the case with most of the few unfortunates who ever did.

'To cut long story short, Pa found no gold in Velarde's canyon, nor let Loco Louey cut his throat, but he did find Consuela, our mama,' Melissa said.

Her dark eyes shone with the excitement and romance of her story. 'Pa infatuated with her beauty. He very smart. He tricked Loco Louey into selling her to him for worthless treasure map to lost mine. They make quick escape over Border to Highgrade Pocket at time of big gold rush. "Son-of-an-anglo-bitch!" say Louey, but never catch him.'

'So you reckon your pa ain't all bad,' Drift said.

Melissa reflected, trying to find a word.

'He ornery – possessive. Maybe he lost some mind when Mama died. He not leave place where they so happy, even though it now only ghost town.'

Drift was still of the opinion the girls would be better off someplace else. But Mad Dan was one mean bastard. He wouldn't stand still for their quitting. If it happened, he'd be fit to be tied. As for any fellow taking them off, you could bet he wouldn't allow that, either. It'd come to shooting. Always had, they did tell.

'Your father treats you and your sister bad. Real bad.'

'Pa say he glad you dead. You bring hides from Box V. It a plot to tar him cow-thief, he say.' Melissa scowled. 'What you got against Pa?'

Drift's face heated. He felt guilty.

'The hides make no difference at the end of the day,' he blustered. 'Everyone on the Box V knows Mad Dan's been cutting its fences, running its stock. A few head here; a few there. Damn' nuisance. If a few hides and some lime is what it takes to bring the scoundrel to book, it's all right with me!'

Melissa jumped up in agitation, all fiery as was her wont when she encountered what she saw as unfairness.

'Man who rustle cows not Pa!'

'Then who in the devil's name is it? Ain't no one else thisaways.'

'It man from Box V who do it. I seen. I watch.'

'Is that a fact?' Drift said wonderingly. He knew the ghost town girl had a keen eye and came and went though the woods like she was a spirit herself. 'What Box V man?'

'Big man. Tall man with hard face. He wear two guns tied down on legs. A shootist, I think. He act like boss man.'

Drift was staggered. This was a turn-up.

His brain raced. 'What does he do with the cows?'

'He sell them to passing scum – badmen who ride through fast on way to Border and Old Mexico. They give him much *dinero* ... greenbacks, gold. They real friendly. Call him "Zack". Shake his hand. It' – she searched for the word – 'organized, I think. Sometime he bring those fellows horses, too, to change for tired ones.'

Drift shook his spinning head. 'By God! Zack Emmett stealing from the Box V...'

'But you in with him,' Melissa stated matter-of-factly, surprised by his shocked response.

'The hell I ain't!' he protested. 'This needs some thinking on.'

It also called for action, which he couldn't give. His frustration at his forced sojourn on the mountain grew hugely in one leaping bound.

Zack Emmett's infamy had to be exposed to Kiliaen Van Dam. It was also imperative that Emmett's plans for Rebecca were stopped. The idea that Big Dutch's pretty daughter could be hitched to the treacherous range boss was an abomination.

'I've gotta get back to the Box V!' he shouted in exasperation.

Melissa looked at him gravely. 'You poor fool! You go nowhere till leg better. You read?'

'Do I read? What is this? Of course I read. Being a cowhand doesn't mean I'm dumb.' Drift found it hard to keep up with her mercurial changes of subject.

'I also not dumb, but not know reading.'

Drift realized that what he'd said was tactless. He probably owed his life to the uneducated girl.

'Sorry. I didn't mean to be rude.'

She accepted the gruff apology. 'Maybe I find old book Pa threw out because he no longer want to read. You pass time reading, then you not be so angry about everything.'

Melissa abruptly left him to fret alone.

The storm clouds were surely gathering in every way. Drift shivered as the sun vanished behind an ugly thunderhead piling up over the ravine's towering edge. The wind rose, funnelled by the narrowness of his place of confinement. It whined bleakly through the rocks and the trees, stirred up the dust in gritty clouds, and sent dead leaves in rustling, fleeing hordes along the stream bed.

Melissa was back within what Drift reckoned to be an hour. He noted that this time she wore the red silk neckerchief from Jennings's store in Two Springs. And she brought a water-damaged, leather-bound black volume that was unmistakably a Bible.

She fingered the prize critically, but presented it to him with an air of pride at her handiwork.

'Pa tore out some leaves before he throw whole lot in midden,' she said. 'I put pieces back in book, but maybe not right places. Is that important?'

'I guess I'll be able to figure it out, M'liss,' Drift said. 'Thank you for your kindness. Why did your father throw out the book?

There are men who call it a good book; *the Good Book.*'

She shrugged. 'Pa say it give no answers. It only tease him.'

Melissa didn't tarry this time; she said Mad Dan would be suspicious about her absences.

'Rain come, too. Maybe big storm.' She was suddenly gone like the deer disturbed by an inept hunter.

Drift examined the desecrated Bible, looking to see what he could learn from it. The first two extracted but well-thumbed pages were from the Book of Genesis, 19.

'And Lot went up out of Zoar, and dwelt in the mountain, and his two daughters with him; for he feared to dwell in Zoar: and he dwelt in a cave, he and his two daughters...'

Subsequent verses told how the daughters made the old man drunk with wine and lay with him. *'Thus were both the daughters of Lot with child by their father.'* They bore him sons, Moab and Ben-ammi – *'the same is the father of the children of Ammon unto this day.'*

Drift instantly grasped the significance of the ripped-out pages. He wondered if Mad Dungaree Dan had seen them as some kind of justification for his conduct with Isabella. Or was he aware of the passage's gross debauchery? Could the explicit story over a span of eight verses be read, in fact, without bringing a blush of shame to the cheeks of the reader?

He turned to the other loose leaves. One was from Deuteronomy, 23, where a verse was heavily underscored in pencil:

'An Ammonite or Moabite shall not enter into the congregation of the Lord; even to their tenth generation shall they not enter into the congregation of the Lord for ever...'

It seemed like a clear condemnation of Lot and his daughters; of their incestuous union and its results.

Another chapter, Deuteronomy, 27, railed against all manner of unions: *'Cursed be he that lieth with his father's wife... Cursed be he that lieth with his sister, the daughter of his father, or the daughter of his mother... Cursed be he that lieth with his mother-in-law...'*

But it conspicuously failed to mention own daughters. Did the Bible say nothing specific on such cases?

That must have tantalized Mad Dan, Drift mused. Or was the clincher in the last of the marked pages, on which Leviticus, 18, declared, *'None of you shall approach to any that is near of kin to him, to uncover their nakedness...'*

This soiled page had been violently screwed up at some stage. He imagined Melissa's sure hands carefully restoring the ball to a semblance of its former flatness, removing the crumples in the thin paper and smoothing out the thousand wrinkles. And all the time she would have been un-knowing of the message she was restoring.

Drift couldn't have expected to find himself in a more bizarre situation, doing Bible study in a primitive, wilderness shelter while the sky darkened and the wind rose.

He'd never been an ardent Bible student. From his orphanage days way back, he'd found it fostered a misplaced smugness in folks who did overmuch of it, aside from taking time he'd never had enough of to interpret meanings from the archaic words. But he could understand how to the lonely the Scriptures might become a comfort. Or equally a torment.

Had Mad Dan been troubled by his conscience?

He turned the book over in his hands, examining its pathetic condition closely. The insides were buckled from dampness – maybe, to judge by the extent of the brown stains, an immersion in water. Evidence of mildew clung to parts of the discoloured binding where its complete removal had proven impossible. Flicking the pages dislodged a scaly insect, obscenely shiny and grey, which slithered promptly into new hiding in his rush bedding.

Then the book fell open at the front flyleaf. It carried an inscription in bold handwriting. Though the blue-black ink was faded, and the book's soaking had caused it to run and bleed smudgily into the paper, it remained completely legible.

It said, *'Daniel Garrity, Philadelphia, 1835.'*

12

THE STORM BREAKS

Garrity! His own name, and confirmation of a wild surmise already long held. He needed no firmer evidence than this of the true identity of the hermit of Highgrade Pocket. The hunch that the end of his personal mission would be in this one-time gold-rush district had indeed been correct. Almost by chance, he held the appalling answer in his shaking hands.

What should he do with it?

Ruefully, he recognized once again that he was in no shape to take action when the call for it was like a scream inside his head. Damn his injured leg!

He dragged himself to the opening of the shelter, pulled himself up on to his feet and hobbled a couple of steps. Excruciating pain tore from his left leg to his brain and the sweat beaded on his brow.

It was hot, damnably hot. His nerves were already singing with pain; with his fears for Rebecca and Big Dutch's Box V; with the shattering story told by the sad Bible. His inner tension seemed to offer a perfect conduit for the electricity that charged the outer air. Like attracts like. His hair prickled.

Drift saw that the dark clouds were now everywhere overhead, bringing a false dusk. The whining wind dropped momentarily and in the brush, a nightbird called. More distant, he heard the piteous squeal of a burrow-seeking rabbit ambushed by an edgy mountain cat. And far-off streaks of lightning and low rumbles of distant thunder heralded the coming storm.

Brief spits of rain made dark mini-craters in the absorbing dust. The odd spits quickly became an insistent spatter, and Drift retreated to his shelter, wiping sweat and rain from his face. It was refreshing, but he reckoned a soaking in his present physical state would not be for the best.

After a flash of brighter lightning, thunder rolled at closer quarters, the echoes bouncing back and forth for miles through the rugged peaks and troughs of the mountain landscape. The reverberations travelled, too, through the very rock. It shook like a slumbering monster awakening beneath Drift's feet.

Then the wind returned and with it came the full onslaught of the rainstorm. The spatter became big, hard, driven drops. They rapidly soaked and penetrated the rush cladding of his shelter. He couldn't avoid the cold trickles that sprang into being here, there and everywhere.

He'd get his soaking after all.

He prepared as best he could for an uncomfortable time of it. From his experience of these climes, he knew a rain like this could last for hours, ending the previous season of near-drought.

Outside, the cloudburst produced a roaring cascade that made visibility beyond scant yards an impossible blur. In consequence, Drift didn't know how much the stream that threaded the bottom of the ravine had swollen until its swirling waters lapped at his threshold. In ten minutes, what had been little more than a rill had become a raging torrent.

The movement of the mounting water turned into a rush through the undergrowth. It was both fascinating and frightening. Whole bushes and small saplings were undermined and toppled. Some formed new obstacles at which the water worried doggedly. Others were simply swept away beyond the curtain of the downpour.

Drift decided it was time he quit the shelter and tried to make higher ground. Pelted by the drenching rain, he was soon disabused of any notion that this was possible. Even with the carefully chosen and trimmed stick Melissa had brought him for use as a crutch, his footing was unsteady. The wetted scree upslope did the rest.

He fell, jarring and grazing himself, but worse, he went into an unstoppable slide down the steep and slippery incline.

He snatched at a passing juniper like he was already the proverbial drowning man clutching at a straw. His desperate grasp and added weight were enough to wrench sodden roots from their precarious hold. Man, shrub and a shower of smaller rocks shot into the vicious swirl of the ever-rising river that had formerly been the placid stream.

Drift went under, but hit bottom and pushed up on to his good leg to break the surface. He sucked in air, choking and spitting silty water from his lungs. But his footing was unsteady. He toppled and his head went under the water again and he took a second mouthful.

Never properly on his good foot, Drift was then completely thrown off it, and swept away by the fast current, kicking furiously. Moments later, it spilled him helplessly into a larger body of white water that drove relentlessly into a system of rocky gullies and canyons – the same giant's maze, he guessed, which he'd observed from the old stage road, but now flooded and doubly dangerous.

All kinds of driftwood and greenery were tumbled along on the flood. Terrifyingly, he was in no better position than the inanimate flotsam, a plaything with no control over his fate. But he refused to be daunted yet. While there was life, there was hope.

In this new element, numbed by the chill, and carried weightlessly, Drift was for the first time in days unaware of the pain in his useless leg.

He grabbed at a substantial log, the remnant of an uprooted tree, before it could flash past him. Hauling himself up on it gave him some buoyancy. He spluttered and coughed out more muddy water.

The log was no boat. He had to keep a clutch on the rough bark, since it tried to roll as well as twist and turn in the water's mad flow. But it allowed him to have his head out of the water, to look around.

Causes for greater alarm presented themselves as he and his log hurtled along on the surging, remorseless flood. Waiting fangs of upthrust rock with beards of froth loomed up and vanished at breakneck speed.

And a flash of lightning showed that ahead the angry river was funnelled between the black masses of two constricting walls. At the end of the narrow channel was a boulder-fringed rim – an abrupt falling-away to invisible turbulence below.

The river hurled itself over the rim with unending fury. A great moving screen of spouts and wind-driven spray was tossed up sky-high.

If he came out of this alive, it would be a miracle.

In Highgrade Pocket, Melissa watched the rain slanting down. She stood on the porch of the old brick bank building her father had taken over for their home.

It began, as these events usually did, with a hollow drumming on the bits of rooftop still sound and a rhythmic dripping into eerie emptinesses below. All dust was quickly settled, and from the rotting dryness of the ghost town arose the distinctive odour of long-parched wood and earth when first touched by rain.

Soon, puddles and rivulets formed out in the deserted streets. At intervals, lightning lit up the town for vivid moments and showed the storm to be a regular gully-washer.

The rain continued to fall in unabated sheets for longer than an hour. Melissa's thoughts, which had turned quickly to the stranger she'd lodged in the hide in the ravine, grew increasingly concerned. Then, as the water gurgled around the sturdy bank's foundations, they took a jump to frantic. A block away, another of the weather-greyed falsefronts made its final splintering collapse across the street. The crash shot up a huge splash of mud and water.

Melissa looked around and grabbed up a shovel and her coiled lariat. She went to find Isabella in the room they used as a kitchen.

'Issy! We must go help my cowboy. Hide

surely flooded by now.'

'You're crazy, M'liss,' Isabella said. 'He's not your cowboy and Pa will kill us if he finds out what you've been up to.'

They both knew their father was working on a buckboard spring across at the old blacksmith's shop.

Melissa's dark eyes flashed with withering scorn. 'It not me crazy. It you, soft-brain! We not tell Pa. Boy save me twice. I save him only once. Now time to even score. You must come help, or he die! You not come, maybe I run away to Two Springs – tell town's ladies you make Pa do wicked things, like whore.'

Unwillingly, the submissive Isabella joined her sister, consoled by the reassurance that Mad Dungaree Dan wouldn't try to return from the smithy till the rain had passed over.

Wearing tattered slickers and with the mud sucking at their moccasined feet, they struggled to the ravine, heads bent low against the downpour.

Melissa was horrified to discover the entire place awash. Everywhere there was mad confusion, with trees felled, bushes uprooted and the hide gone. Water continued to pour down the steep sides of the ravine to feed the turbulent flood which swept along the bottom.

At the grim and terrible sight, Isabella backed off dumbstruck. She saw only what looked like a calamity they were too late to prevent.

But Melissa saw no cowboy's body bobbing in the floating debris. From her knowledge of the lie of the land and previous floods, she figured the water gushed from here into Horsehead Canyon. She determined she'd go there to check while any last, slim chance remained that the handsome man who'd rescued her twice was still alive.

'Come on!' she yelled at Isabella above the tumult of wind and rain. 'We go this way!'

Luck had not totally deserted Drift Garrity. His sodden log was caught in a spinning eddy, and it veered toward the largest of the black boulders between which the river poured to an unknown lower level.

Maybe Drift could avoid going over the rapid. Behind the big boulder, a build-up of silt washed down by the flood formed a bar.

He paddled feverishly in a bid to ground the log on the smooth, low mound.

His strenuous efforts were rewarded, but the mud and sand of the bar were not as soft as they looked. Once the log's direction was determined, it moved at high velocity and slammed into the bar with sudden, considerable force.

The impact drove its front end deep into the sand, and despite the rough surface of the bark, Drift lost his grip. He was flung off and carried forward by momentum. Hands spread, he landed face down with a bone-jarring thump on the bar.

Freed of his weight, the log completed a somersault, narrowly missing his head as it passed over him, and splashed back into the churning waters beyond. It was reclaimed by the fast-moving main current and seconds later disappeared from view, hurled over the rapid.

Fresh pain racked Drift's left leg. His chest heaved wheezily from exertion and too many mouthfuls of gritty water. He retched and spat out more of the brackish stuff. For long moments, he sprawled motionless, battered but in one piece. And thankful to be alive.

Though Melissa's splints had been stripped from his leg, his valuable .45 by some curious freak was still lodged in the soggy holster. The rain was slackening somewhat.

But his position remained precarious and he knew he couldn't afford to rest. The sandbar was shifting and changing shape around him. Already the furrow gouged into it by the log was being filled up or washed away by the action of the surrounding water. Before long, the bar would be smooth again and its permanency was dubious; its present solidity deceptive.

Getting to his knees, he crawled to the boulder that had given rise to the temporary haven and looked over.

The floodwaters fell in a roaring cataract to a deadly whirlpool far below. If he'd gone over, he wouldn't have had a prayer. Nobody was likely to survive a plunge into such a seething maelstrom. And if they did, a whole series of rapids lay ahead of them, marked by gleaming lines of foam in the half-light.

The falls' own unending racket diminished the thunder in the black skies. The persistent pounding of sound, added to what he had endured, had him dazed, so it was an effort for him to take further stock.

To either side of the water's passage, walls of rock towered forbiddingly, though on one a steep track of sorts wended down to a broad, rocky bank back upstream apiece. But to reach that shelf he'd have to cross a stretch of water against a strong current he already knew would sweep him away to his doom if he tried. Nor was his unreliable leg any help.

It seemed he was safe, at present, but trapped.

'So what is it I die of? Starvation ... drowning ... lameness...?'

Drift left the line of thought unfinished. He rubbed the back of a raw-knuckled hand across his dripping eyebrows to brush away the wet and narrowed his gaze on the track descending the cliff to the promontory. Two slicker-clad figures were picking their way down.

When they reached the shelf of rock, the first flung off its slicker. Any uncertainty Drift had was ended by his glimpse of a bright red neckerchief. Melissa!

She displayed no lack of understanding about what was needed. Drift realized she must have viewed his predicament from the rim of the canyon and had figured out exactly what action she was going to take.

She threw aside the shovel she carried – it was plain he didn't have to be dug out of a landslide – and slipped off the coiled lariat she'd lugged along over her shoulder. She whirled the rope round her head and sent it snaking out toward him over the rushing floodwaters.

171

The first cast fell short, but she rapidly hauled the rawhide in and tried again.

The noose sailed out and up over Drift. He extended his right arm, big hand spread wide to catch it. Cold wet fingers snapped closed like the jaws of a trap. The rope slipped through them ... then he had it gripped. Using both hands, he slipped the noose over his head and down to waist level where he tightened the knot so it couldn't undo.

On the bank, Melissa wound the rope's free end around a spur of rock as effectively as he might dally it himself around a saddle horn. She gave it a tug, demonstrating it was made fast.

Tentatively, Drift waded off the sandbar, wincing as his injured leg complained at the weight he put on it.

'What matter?' Melissa called. 'You run out of nerve?'

'No!' he shouted back. 'My foot's already gone black to the toes with the bruising from the leg. I gotta be careful.'

172

As soon as he was waist deep, he kicked off the bottom and began hauling himself hand over hand up the rope.

He felt like he was waging a tug-of-war against the powerful pull of the flood. Bits of debris hurtling downstream buffeted his head and arms, dealing him new bruises and abrasions. But he clung to the rope; kept on working at moving along it.

He knew the stake here was his life.

13

UNMASKED!

Drift's cow-roper shoulders had muscle enough in them to do the job, but the coldness of the water numbed his hands. Several times his grip on the rope slipped and he was nearly plucked off. His head went under the water repeatedly.

Yet after what seemed an eternity, he made the rocky shelf where the two girls were and crawled up on to it. He coughed and spluttered indecorously. He groaned as they helped him to his feet and freed him from the lariat.

'How do you feel?' Melissa asked.

'Thanks to you, I'm still alive,' he gasped. 'I'd've been a goner there sooner or later, that's the truth.'

She had a tight, triumphant smile. 'Then we equal now. You save me from Jennings and bear when you not have to.'

'Pshaw! I don't much care for dirty store-keepers and riled bears anyhow.'

Isabella was looking ever more agitated. 'Hurry, M'liss. Leave him now. It's getting dark and Pa will find us gone.'

Melissa shot her sister a dark look full of contempt. 'We can't leave cowboy here. We must help him now to new, dry hideout in town.'

Isabella was distraught. 'Then Pa will find him,' she wailed. 'We'll be punished for sure. He'll be *killed*.'

Drift patted his holstered revolver. 'Maybe I'll have something to say about that. 'Sides, I've a notion to have words with your pa. Some questions to put to him.'

Since it was unknown to him whether the soaked cartridges in his .45 would fire or not, he was less certain about his chances than he tried to sound.

But his bold talk dealt a mortal blow to

the last vestiges of Isabella's courage. With a final inarticulate wail, she turned heel and fled back up the steep track to the rim as fast as conditions would allow.

'Isabella!' Melissa cried, but was ignored. She turned back to Drift. 'Oh, damn!'

Drift shrugged. 'I scared her, I guess. My mistake.'

'You make big one this time!'

'Don't take on about it so. I'll cope.'

Melissa sighed. 'It difficult for me alone to help you limp to town. Also, it risky to hide you in town if Isabella decide to tell.'

'When the time comes, I'm gonna have to face your pa anyhow, and I reckon that's all right with me, too. It's called having to take your chances.'

'This fighting talk,' Melissa said, frowning. 'Why you want to fight?'

'That's for me to know, and you to be told by your pa. I aim to make him tell, and it'll be none too soon.'

Even so, Drift was coldly, disparagingly angry with himself. He should have been more careful about how he'd handled the downtrodden Isabella. His ordeal had led him to speak out too openly, too quickly to the girls. Which could prove to have been foolish.

'Do you think Issy will talk?'

He'd confused Melissa. She said worriedly, 'It possible. She scared white.'

Although the storm had abated a little, it was far from over. A flash of lightning showed low, massive thunderheads still looming over the black rim and rain continued to fall and sweep down the sides of the ravine to feed the seething flood from which Drift had been rescued.

The town seemed the only option for shelter and a hideout. Drift himself knew of nowhere else within miles, and it seemed Melissa didn't either.

'We have to be very, very watchful,' she said.

Drift hobbled, Melissa walked up the track that clung to the side of the ravine. They went side by side where its width permitted, Melissa supporting him. In other places, he used the shovel as a crutch.

The rim reached, a further half-hour's slow travel in similar mode brought them to the outskirts of Highgrade Pocket.

The proper darkness of night had fallen, and Drift hoped this, with the softness of the ground under their feet and the continuing rain, would cover their stealthy entry to the deserted old settlement.

Somewhere above the scudding clouds the moon had risen, and a diffused greyness lay over the town. The grey broke into vivid white and black with the occasional flash of lightning. The desolate scene was for passing moments starkly lit up, and then it returned to gloom, accompanied by muted rolls of thunder as the storm retreated into the canyon country.

Drift jumped at the first revealing flash, and who could blame him? He'd never seen a place so dismal and forbidding. So dangerous-looking.

Loose boards swayed and flapped and

creaked in the wind. Water poured through holed roofs to splash into echoing vacancies, inhabitable for sure by rodents only. Few windows still had whole panes of glass. Most held none or only broken shards, and the frames were rotten. Weeds sprouted in unexpected places. Boardwalks had collapsed and once-imposing falsefronts sagged in splinters across them. At a stage before disintegration had been so advanced, someone had nailed rough-sawn lengths of lumber across the doors and windows of various buildings, perhaps to bar entry by vagrants and ransackers – an effort futile and long abandoned.

Here and there a sun-faded sign, with the lettering scarcely legible, announced some long-gone business enterprise ... a feed merchant's, a gunsmith's, a bakery.

Drift began to understand how Melissa and Isabella, the ghost town belles, had come to be regarded as the only attractions the place had left for the men who knew of the Pocket.

How could the girls live here other than as prisoners?

He felt a wild urge to find a mount – even the slowest and balkiest mule would do – to saddle up and ride away forever, fleeing all the ruin, cruelty and hatred he knew lay buried here just beneath the surface. And which it had been his intention to expose.

Melissa steered him to the ruins of the marshal's office at the opposite end of town to the bank where Mad Dungaree Dan had made his den. The office had been constructed more solidly than most of the Pocket's buildings.

Inside, were a built-in bunk, a couple of crippled chairs, old reward posters peeling from the walls, and most promisingly a rusty stove that looked as though it still might be serviceable. He'd be glad of the chance to dry out some of his wet clothing and still his chattering teeth with a good blaze.

'It have to be done at night, or Pa see smoke from stove pipe,' Melissa warned. 'I bring you pot and coffee, too. A little lamp oil.'

'That would be good,' Drift said, nodding slowly. 'I think I can handle it from here on.'

He didn't add his private thoughts that this thing had to be brought to a head. That he'd not only come to the Pocket at the behest of Zack Emmett – he'd also had a personal objective. He'd always been aware that the time had to come for confirmation, even confrontation, and he'd planned for it to do so.

Until Melissa had brought him the Bible, thus ending all doubts, the settling of the business had been frustratingly but at the same time comfortably remote. Now, suddenly, the reckoning was at hand.

Mad Dungaree Dan was a mountain wolf whom he'd chosen to hunt down as a rancher might the solitary grey beast that fed itself by attacking his defenceless stock.

Melissa hovered, puzzled and as though in two minds. She was clearly torn between staying with him, maybe to ask questions, and returning to the bank building where her continued absence could be a problem.

She went all at once, as was her way. First she was there, then she wasn't, and Drift was alone with his troubled mind.

But not for long.

When the object of his hatred made his sudden entrance, Drift was not prepared for the surprise of it. He was feeding bits of broken lumber – the less passable of the two chairs – to the fire Melissa had lit in the stove. Then, above the steady drumming of the rain, a thud of boots and the scrape of a slumped door on warped floorboards grabbed his attention.

He dropped the stove lid. His hand snaked to his holstered .45. Just as quickly, it froze. The ominous click of a thumbed-back hammer fell on his ears.

'Wouldn't were I you, boy,' Mad Dungaree Dan said. 'Lift 'em – not too high – that's dandy. Now turn aroun' prop'ly... Slow.'

Drift raised his hands, chest high, and pivoted carefully toward the voice.

A flash of lightning gave its stark illumination to the tableau. The old man faced him with drawn and cocked Yellowboy carbine. A shabby buffalo coat was draped over his humped shoulders, wet and smelly from the rain. His eyes glinted with madness. Or was it just the weird, blueish flickering of the storm?

Behind him was Isabella, face corpsewhite and taut, and behind her, Melissa – all flushed and wildly bedraggled and looking kind of mad at everything, maybe herself included.

Drift's heart lurched and a cold, sick feeling gripped his stomach. His mouth went dry. So Mad Dan had found him so soon!

He guessed he'd been betrayed – probably with defensive intent by Isabella; possibly inadvertently by the skittish Melissa. It didn't really matter which.

He licked his lips. In a voice edged with bitterness, he said, 'You can send me straight to hell if you want, old man, but it won't make your own sins the easier to answer for. And the day *you* get there, I'll be waiting to stoke up the fires. You think long about that.'

Mad Dan chewed on his lower lip, working his bristled jaw. From the growth of greying beard it looked like his last shave had been given by the barber on that seemingly long-ago day in Two Springs.

'Think about what, cowpoke?' The bright eyes fixed him with a searching scrutiny from the weathered face. 'I reck'n yuh're jest a dirty, skirt-chasin' rustler, 'bout to git his needin's!'

Drift grinned mirthlessly and shook his head.

'Not so. And I'll give you and your girls plenty to think on before you blow me away. I've gotten the straight of your rotten, selfish life, *Daniel Garrity!*'

The harshly spoken name was totally unexpected by the man whom all and sundry had called nothing but Dungaree Dan, or Mad Dan.

Shiftiness narrowed Mad Dan's gaze; the

carbine wavered but held level at waist height.

'What yuh blatherin' 'bout, yuh damned dirty saddle-tramp? The Pocket's a long way inta wild country to come lookin' fer trouble.'

'Maybe so, but it ain't far enough for a bigamist and cheat to hide away from the truth.'

It was the hermit's turn to lick his lips. 'I don't know what yuh're talkin' 'bout,' he maintained loudly, but his certainty was unconvincing.

'Sure you do. Your memory can't be that bad, though it's been nigh on twenty-five years. I'm telling the story of your stinking life how you know it really is.'

Melissa pushed past her white-faced sister, but kept a wary eye that she didn't step in front of her pa's threatening carbine.

'Drift! I not understand. What you say to Pa?'

'I'm saying he's my pa, too. And you're my half-sister.'

14

GUNPLAY IN THE POCKET

Drift poured out the whole story. Melissa was engrossed. Her expression changed from blank incredulity to as much of an understanding as she was capable.

'Mad Dan had a family before he met your mother. His real name is Garrity – Daniel Garrity,' Drift explained. 'Mine is Alexander Garrity, and like I said I'm his son. Many years ago Daniel left Philadelphia to look for gold.'

'Phila-dare-fear...? What that?' the girl asked.

'A place back East. A city, which is like a big town.'

'Ah, yes. Like Two Springs. Like High-grade Pocket many seasons gone.'

186

Drift didn't try to expand her limited perception. He pressed on.

'And he left in that city his lawful wife and the baby boy who was myself. Later, he met Consuela Cavara. Besotted, he then cruelly broke off all contact he had with his kin. Letters no longer came. News nor money neither. The true wife's health failed under the strains of extreme poverty. Thusly, abandonment condemned the poor woman to die of want, while I was put in an orphanage.

'My lot there was a grim one. What little comforts orphanage youngsters are given come out of the charity of strangers. You go to bed with a half-filled belly. You wake to dirty chores, harsh discipline and fights with your fellow inmates for the scant reliefs such a life offers.

'I ran away many times. Each time they brought me back to a thrashing for my ingratitude.'

Melissa uttered a gasp of horror. 'This terrible! You should have found mountain –

good place to hide. I never thought of Pa having life and kinfolks other than ones here at Highgrade Pocket. It hard to understand.'

Mad Dan jerked his Yellowboy. 'Who else've yuh told this pile o' horse droppin's?'

'Nary a soul. I got self-respect, even if you haven't, *sir*.' Drift laid sarcastic emphasis on the respectful address. 'Eventually, my growing was done and I was out of there and into a world that offered me no prospects of advancement, no connections or entry to the good things in civilized Eastern life. Like others in those circumstances I went West and became a cowboy.

'Looked at from afar, it had seemed romantic and adventurous. Well, believe you me, it ain't neither. Oft-times, it's hard, rough and through-and-through dirty.'

Mad Dan growled, 'Nobody made yuh do what yuh didn't want to do; go where yuh didn't want to go. An' I don't know nothin' 'bout no Garrity feller...'

Drift scoffed at the barefaced lie.

'Sure you do. I've learned it from the

daughters given you by the beautiful Mexican woman you stole from Loco Louey. In life, she turned your head; in death, she turned your wits. Now you're plumb loco – a dirty, unprincipled deserter who's sunk again to abusing his own flesh and blood. And this time it's maybe worse. You're content to live right where you can see the cruel results of your selfish behaviour!'

He'd struck now at Mad Dan's deepest secret, hinting at knowledge of his unnatural practices and his immorality. The oldster's shock, maybe anger, at the exposure caused the carbine to waver again.

So when the aim of the Yellowboy's muzzle shifted fractionally away from Drift, to the right, he took a chance. He sprang to the left and completed the instinctive draw of his Colt revolver that the ghost town trio's arrival had sparked and aborted. Both men now had a gun in their hands, though Drift didn't know whether the loads in his, soaked in the flood, would be effective.

Melissa and Isabella screamed in earsplitting unison.

But neither man could bring himself to pull a trigger. A paralysis gripped them alike.

Bleakly, Drift saw how he couldn't escape with his own character untainted if the man who'd sired him were to meet a bloody downfall. For years, he'd longed for this moment of retribution in which he'd denounce his despicable father. Yet at its coming he felt only a sudden coldness and emptiness in his heart. He was stilled by no trace of a fear of his death, just by despair.

His gunspeed might let him claim his vengeance, though possibly at his own life's cost. But what would happen to the two damaged girls who'd helped him survive his mountain foray after he'd killed the man who was a parent of all of them?

What would happen to himself?

The struggle with his demons wasn't over. He still had them to overcome before he could accept his mission was over; his cause won; his courage proven, physically, morally and spiritually.

Mad Dan recovered first. 'I figgered as much,' he grated sneeringly. 'Galahad to the rescue of the pretty ladies – but he ain't got the sand to try an' gun me down!'

'Not a bit of it, old man. Maybe I don't shoot you like the cur-dog you are for the good of your uncleansed soul.'

Mad Dan was rising to no bait. He jerked his head toward the door and addressed his girls. 'Issy! M'liss! Get yuh disobedient selfs home, will yuh?'

He kept his beady gaze on Drift. 'As fer you, cowboy pup, I suggests yuh foller 'em, if'n yuh ain't too big fer your britches to do what's best.'

Drift gestured at the parlous amenities of the broken-down peace office and forced a grin he didn't feel like. 'Guess I will at that. Ain't much in the way of comforts to keep a man here. If this half-busted leg lets me, I'll move on in the morning.'

He didn't add that he might again try to persuade Melissa and Isabella to go with him. Maybe he could enlist Rebecca Van

Dam's help in placing his half-sisters some-where civilized. Safe.

The mutterings and grumblings of the storm were retreating into the wilder reaches of the mountains, but rain was still falling, further obscuring their hurried passage through the darkness to the more substantial shelter of the old brick bank building.

Therefore, it was fortunately not until they'd almost reached it that they were spotted.

'Somethin' movin' over there!' a voice rapped from behind what still stood of the livery barn.

Drift recognized it – Lew Feffer, his tricky, so-called new pard from the Box V.

'It's all of 'em!' another speaker said. Maybe it was Pete. 'The gals an' Mad Dan, an' Drift Garrity with 'em ... with guns!'

'Shuddup!' Zack Emmett broke in. Then he hollered at the four on the street. 'You there! Hold hard! We're here to make sure of you rustlin' bastards – usin' lead if needs be!'

Mad Dan and his daughters were taken aback, but Drift knew what was going on in an instant.

Under cover of the storm, the Box V were making good on their plan to stage a raid. They'd take Highgrade Pocket by force, frame Mad Dan for the rustling – which Drift now knew to be the work of the crooked range boss – and do as they wanted with the girls.

He cried, 'M'liss, Issy! Keep a-going! Right on into the bank!'

Scared by the strange and threatening voices, the girls needed no second bidding. They bolted inside.

'Stop 'em! Don't let 'em make a standoff of this!' Emmett bellowed.

But it was too late to lay hands on the girls, and when two foolhardy members of his bunch broke from spread-out places of concealment in the shadows, Mad Dan promptly went to shooting with his trusty Yellowboy.

One Box V hand went down with a high-pitched screech as a heavy slug shattered his kneecap. He collapsed, moaning and writhing in the mud. Blood spurted at a gruesome rate through the hands he clutched to his leg.

The other man darted back out of the line of fire as Mad Dan worked the lever on the carbine and swung on him to take a second shot.

Angry red flashes split the darkness all around as Box V guns opened up.

Drift limped after Mad Dan into the bank. He felt a cold, gurgling sickness rising in his stomach. Lead spattered the mud about his clumsy feet and ricocheted off the bank's brick walls but, astonishingly, they made cover without stopping one of the hail of bullets.

'These goddamn gunnies friends o' yours, boy?' Mad Dan asked.

'Thought some of 'em were. Now, I ain't too sure.'

Beyond a firm conviction that he should save the girls, Drift was in a quandary. With whom did he throw in his lot?

Where should his loyalties lie? With his crafty, miscreant father who preyed sexually on one of his half-sisters? Or with the violent Box V bunch whose leader would probably take the first opportunity presented to wipe out his rivalry for Rebecca, heiress to the Van Dam herds and lands?

'Waal,' Mad Dan rasped, flinging off the dirty buffalo coat, 'we'll be ready for 'em. M'liss, give the cowpoke that ol' Sharps, will yuh?'

'I got my Colt,' Drift said. 'And I don't know that I want to take sides in any gun battle.'

Mad Dan spat into a big open fireplace.

'Gawd almighty, boy! These gents're a-gunnin' fer us both, an' ain't lookin' none fer your say-so. They's dealt yuh cards in the game already. The tricks they aims to win is my purdy gals.'

Drift suspected that Mad Dan, though a one-eyed maniac, relished the discomfiture of his high-and-mighty accuser. He could

195

only regret the odd turn of events that had allied them without choice.

Uncharacteristically sullen, Drift took up position to one side of the bank's broken and part-boarded front window. Mad Dan had gone to the other.

Melissa darted across to him and leaned an old Sharps against the wall beside him.

'Use long gun, Drift,' she said.

Drift ignored the entreaty and hefted his Colt half-heartedly.

'They've got us pinned down here,' he said. 'How long can we hold out? How much ammo you got?'

No one answered his questions.

At first glance, the town looked empty. Mad Dan's shooting had spooked the raiders, but he could hear Zack Emmett yelling out orders, though actual words were indistinct.

Silence, except for the patter and drip of rain. Then, furtive movements in the shadows across the Street. The scuffling splash of running boots through puddles.

Patiently, Mad Dan waited for a target.

When a Box V man darted from an alley, headed for some new position, the oldster lifted carbine to shoulder. It roared in his hands and recoiled against him as he squeezed the trigger. The quick shot was placed with frightening accuracy, taking the fast-moving figure high in the right body.

The cowhand threw up his arms and slipped over in the main drag's mud. Drift heard the hit man grunt and curse in pain. He crawled back into the darkness like a scuttling crab, sobbing and moaning, swearing at his sidekicks for failing to give him covering fire.

Another respite.

Plainly, Emmett was having trouble with firing up his men to stage a concerted attack. Mad Dan's reputation for protecting his fillies with his carbine, now backed firsthand by an accurate demonstration, had them treed.

From the sounds of it, after the second man was wounded, a heated discussion ensued. In the hulking ruins around the bank, terse words were shouted to and fro.

Then a flutter of white appeared from between the facing ruins. It was followed cautiously by an arm. When Mad Dan held his fire, Zack Emmett showed, advancing slowly, waving a cloth.

Mad Dan cackled. 'Looks like some bastard musta shucked his longjohns!'

Emmett reached mid-point of the wide street and was within earshot.

'Hold hard!' Mad Dan shouted. 'That's fur enough. Say your piece!'

Emmett bawled back, 'It's this damn' foolishness that's gone far enough. Come out, cow-thief! You're boxed. Give yourself up an' you'll be spared.'

'Oh yeah?' Mad Dan jeered. 'What guarantee do I git? An' how 'bout m' gals?'

'We can't negotiate with you in there,' Emmett objected. 'I can't hear what you're sayin'. Meet me out here, Dungaree Dan. I've no gun in my hand, I'll come no closer, and my crew'll stay back.'

Melissa protested, 'Don't trust bad man, Pa! You step out, he riddle you with bullets, he come get us.'

Drift didn't like it either. He'd seen the swiftness of Emmett's draw. He knew the range boss was an ex-gunslick. Mad Dan was smart with his carbine, but he was no professional shootist.

Yet the present situation was a stalemate and the longer it went on, the less chance there was that the four in the bank would survive. They were cornered in the old building like rats.

Mad Dan said fiercely to his companions, 'We gotta finish this in short order.' Lifting his voice, he said, 'All right, mister. I come out, an' yuh can state your business, but I'll have m' Yellerboy ready, mind.'

'Stop!' Drift rapped, the voice of doubt shrieking warning within him. 'You need to watch out here, old man. You're taking a damn' big chance.' Then he, too, called out louder:

'Zack Emmett! This is Drift Garrity. Tell

your men to step out in the street where we can see 'em! The old man ain't gonna walk out in front of no hidden firing squad.'

Emmett's stance seemed to tighten. He was displeased by Drift's intervention.

'Sure,' he said at last with a shrug. 'But you better remember whose side you're on, Garrity. Miss Rebecca was beside herself when she learned how you'd gone up on the mountain, to hunt out the rustler. We're here at her instigation, you might say.'

Emmett gave orders for his men to show themselves. As they shuffled into view, Drift knew it would serve no long-term purpose to try to dissuade Mad Dan. His reprobate father had a mind of his own, weighing everything in some balance that didn't give what normal men would call honest results.

Assured of his own canniness, the oldster swaggered defiantly out the door.

'See, mister? I ain't bashful none–'

'Get back, Dan! Sniper ... it's a trap!'

Drift screamed the warning, and in the same split-second took aim with his .45 at the black silhouette of a man and rifle. His raking glance had suddenly detected the ominous shapes rising against the moon-greyed clouds on the highest part of the tumbledown structure opposite.

But the crouching sniper had already drawn his bead, and a livid streak of flame stabbed down toward the street, accompanied by the whiplash crack of a Winchester.

The bullet smashed into Mad Dan's middle, staggering him and causing him to drop the carbine. He clutched at his stomach, and his legs gave way under him.

He fell into a foetal position in the mud.

15

IN THE BLOOD

Drift fired back into the rifleman's muzzle blast.

The sneak shooter rose up with a cry, dropping the gun, which plunged into a puddle far below with a splash and a thud. The man proceeded to fold slowly forward, till he tumbled off his high perch.

On his way down, he hit the rusted remnant of an awning made from roofing iron. He bounced with a resounding boom, and was dead when he struck the ground.

Melissa rushed from the bank to her father's side. Isabella hovered uncertainly on the steps.

'Bastards!' Melissa screamed and seized up the dropped Yellowboy.

Before she could bring it to bear, Zack Emmett kicked it from her hands, then grabbed hold of her.

Drift rushed forward. 'Let her go, Emmett! She ain't got the gun now and she can help me get Mad Dan back inside. We have to do what we can for him.'

Emmett sneered. 'Very touching, very gallant. But he looks pretty bad to me. Gut shot.'

Mad Dan's hands were stained with the blood pulsing out through a hole low in the bib of his dungarees. His eyes were expressionless, glassy.

Drift considered soberly what thoughts, if any, might be going through Mad Dan's mind as death surely drew close to carry him away. This time, his folly would take him to a place from where he couldn't return, ever.

Emmett glowered, but Drift pushed past him to the dying old man's side.

Drift had already holstered his Colt. He didn't reckon he was in that bad with the

Box V crowd that his former pards would shoot him down in cold blood. Zack Emmett doubtless had motives of his own for wishing him dead, but he was scarcely likely to act on them openly, before witnesses. A stray shot in some sort of ruckus was one thing; informal execution another.

As for Drift's killing of Mad Dan's would-be assassin, the sniper had shot first from hiding. Fair men's code would say he'd known the risks he was handling in a dirty play, had thought he had the odds beat, and had gotten his deserts.

Isabella joined Drift and Melissa and together the three of them carried their barely conscious father into the place he'd made his unconventional home. Melissa rushed for water and cloths to attend to the bloody wound.

Emmett followed them in.

Drift said, 'Stay out of here, for God's sake!'

'I didn't hear you say that, Garrity,' Emmett said. 'I'm warnin' you, we're none too rapt with how you're handlin' yourself here.'

'You're getting your way, ain't you?' Drift said. He straightened up as best he could on a bad leg and faced him, glaring. 'Mad Dan's smeared to hell and gone for the rustling, and in no shape to answer charges.'

'Sure ain't fit to string up,' Emmett allowed.

Drift was full of scorn. 'I figure it was your idea to plug him under protection of a white flag, boss. Smart stunt!'

'Now see here, kid, that's no tone to take. Me an' the boys are comin' in here accordin' to plan. The ol' man's a goner an' you can't talk us out of it.'

Melissa was following the exchange, but it was beyond her comprehension. She paused in her ministrations to her pa and asked Drift, 'You make bad men pay?'

Emmett guffawed and did the answering before Drift could frame an understandable reply.

'Naw, darlin'. It's been a mighty long wait, but it's you an' your sweet sister that's doin' the payin'.'

His lusting eyes travelled over her young body. The beautifully rounded lines were shown to fullest advantage as she crouched by the dying man, her short skirt way up above her knees.

Drift said, 'Don't listen to him! You don't have to do anything for the murdering skunks.'

Emmett raised his voice. 'Come on in, boys! Garrity's forgot the score. We get to have ourselves a good time with the ghost town belles – all untasted an' ripe for the takin'!'

With an ugly laugh, he shouldered Drift aside and dragged Melissa to her feet.

'Stop it!' she cried. 'Are you crazy?'

'Yeah ... crazy 'bout gettin' the dirty clothes offa yuh!'

She resisted furiously. 'What meaning of this? You rape us?'

'You'll find out!' Emmett growled. Box V rannies crowded into the room to give him a hand – and she was more than several handfuls.

Strong and healthy, Melissa spat, kicked and scratched. One man gave up, yelling and cursing in agony after he'd torn his hand free from her sharp bite.

'Treat her rough as you like, boys,' Emmett urged. 'Nothin's barred.'

Meanwhile, others of the bunch fell on Isabella. The elder girl was a different case altogether. She went limp. Docile, whimpering and white-faced scared, she let them tear at her clothes in their haste to have their way with her.

Despite Melissa's desperate struggles, she was flung to the floor. A pack of panting, sweaty men piled on to her, intent on her ravishing.

All attention diverted, Drift snatched out his gun and turned it on Zack Emmett. He shouted at the top of his voice, above the hubbub of the excited aggressors and the contrasting fury and distress of their two victims.

'Hold it, the lot of you! Or Emmett gets it. Back off and leave my – the girls alone.' He still hesitated to reveal Melissa and Isabella were his half-sisters and his rescuers from death by drowning.

'The girls are my friends,' he went on, 'as sinned against by Mad Dan as any of us, including myself.'

'What the hell are yuh up to, Drift?' Lew Feffer demanded, misreading the situation. 'We saved yuh from the ol' man. Ain't this the way it was supposed to be? It's owed us by these cow-thievin' hicks.'

Drift laid it out straight.

'No, it ain't owed you. It's Zack Emmett who's the Box V's cow-thief, running off stock for selling to outlaws taking the trail to the Border through the mountains. Putting the blame on an old man. An insane and evil man, I'll allow, but not your rustler.'

'I'll be damned,' someone said.

Emmett first tried to bluff his way around Drift's allegations. 'Pay no heed, boys. Garrity's got the facts here all wrong.'

Drift wagged his revolver. 'No, Emmett, I got you dead to rights. It's been witnessed.

You've been up to a helluva lot of mischief in these parts, two-timing on Big Dutch and Miss Rebecca in every way. It's time you were stopped.'

He put his reliance on his listeners being ordinary cowpunchers, men like himself. With the exception of the one-time gunslinger Emmett, they were men who would handle a rope and a branding iron, throw a steer, and ride hard. They weren't by inclination traitors, cheaters and bullies. Nor killers and rapists.

With his next words, Drift threw himself open to their judgement. 'I appeal to the rest of you as my pardners and friends to–'

Emmett broke in with a derisive laugh.

'Friends! Ain't this rich, fellers? Sounds to me mighty like Garrity's welshin' on arrangements with an unproven windy – a pile o' manure in point of fact. He'll spoil your fun so he can keep it for hisself.'

'That's a lie! I'll take no part in attacking innocents,' Drift said stoutly. 'Nor will any honourable man who counts himself my pal.'

Distaste pulled at Emmett's cruel mouth as he redirected his gaze intently on Drift.

'Now listen to me, Garrity. You won't find no pals here. There ain't friends in our kinda life – you take what you want or it's taken from you. So you let us do as we will. You're through at the Box V. You can get out now if you want, but if you prefer to go to hell, we've more 'n enough guns to accommodate you. You can't stand us all off – not alone.'

Every cowpuncher's eye was fixed on the pair. Thoughts revolved in heads like whirligigs. Who was right? Who should they back? *Who would win?*

Drift licked his lips. Although he covered Emmett with his .45, he knew the other man was hell on wheels at a draw, and that he himself would be no sure winner in a gun duel, let alone a winner after that if it did come to a shootout with the rest over the girls.

What was the likelihood he'd collect a bellyful of lead if he fired on Emmett?

'I've got a lame leg and no horse,' he said

210

after long seconds.

'Too bad,' Emmett drawled. 'We'll give you ten minutes to hobble away.'

Drift kept his eyes fixed on Emmett, but his focus was the whole room and what he saw going on there. The moment had come to take his chance. Emmett was as off-guard as he was ever going to be before the palaver was done with.

'I don't want 'em!' he snapped. At the same time, he threw himself aside, dropped on to his sound knee and triggered his six-gun.

Sick dread rose in his throat as he saw his wild shot had missed. Moreover, Emmett had palmed his own right-hand gun light-ning-fast. In one smooth movement, he cocked, aimed and fired.

The pain in Drift's left shoulder came simultaneously with the boom of Emmett's gun. He was hit!

He fired back but his second try merely sliced the side of Emmett's ribs. The old banking hall rang with the shots. Gunsmoke swirled and added its reek to the noisome atmosphere of the hermit's den.

But Drift exulted. No one else had lifted a gun. And best of all, the development that had decided him on taking his chance was coming to its climax.

Left forgotten in agony, with his life's blood seeping through Melissa's pad of crude bandages and into the filthy floorboards, Mad Dungaree Dan had eased out a bowie knife from under his overalls.

The oldster's fingers trembled as they sought to grasp the haft under the brass handguard, as discoloured as the metal on his old Yellowboy. The bowie's blade looked wickedly sharp, ten inches long, sharpened on one side only to the curve of the tip, but then sharpened on both sides to the point.

The mad glitter had returned for what was surely one last time to the old man's eyes.

With a screech of rage, Drift's dying father propelled himself unsteadily on to his feet and made a lunge at Zack Emmett's back – blood spurting out of his belly, knife grimly gripped and going before.

The range boss had lifted his pistol at arm's length and was pointing it very deliberately at Drift's head. He was about to eliminate the pesky grub-line rider for all time.

Just before Emmett squeezed the trigger, the bowie buried itself to the handguard in his back.

Drift gritted his teeth, ignoring the pain in his shoulder. He turned his gun on the main body of the Box V hands, but with Zack Emmett in his death throes, blood coming out of his mouth, all the fight and carnal appetite was gone out of them.

Zack Emmett's brutal face was contorted with total disbelief. He couldn't see the knife stuck in his back, but he knew he'd been pierced to the lungs by Mad Dungaree Dan in a final piece of resolute craziness before the doomed old man became what looked like a crumpled heap of rags.

Emmett coughed up the choking red in

horrific splatters. He knew he was drowning in his own blood.

'Bastard's kilt me!' he gasped.

Then the look of astonishment was washed way by the pallid blankness of death. His eyes remained open and staring. No one bothered to close them.

In the morning, they buried the dead in Highgrade Pocket's boot hill under a clearing sky. No one saw fit to hump the bodies back to the Box V or Two Springs. The killings were outside the jurisdiction of any local peace officer.

Melissa gathered wild meadow flowers – bunches of showy scarlet paintbrush, yellow Mormon tea and purple-and-white velvet lupins. She placed them on the mound of stones that marked Mad Dan's last resting place.

She urged her sister to do the same. 'Come, Issy, find flowers. He was Pa.'

But the sombre Isabella wouldn't.

Drift was a poor help in the burial chores. His leg was improving by the day, but he now also had a bullet wound in his shoulder that needed better attention than the first-aid the ghost town girls and the Box V hands could offer.

On the borrowed horse of Emmett's dead sniper, he joined the line of riders that picked its way out of the Pocket and on to the old stage road down to the flats and Two Springs.

Melissa and Isabella chose to go with him, freed from the oppressive rule of their deranged father but full of uncertainty about their future.

Isabella, especially, needed help. While her spunkier sister clenched the mules' reins and drove their buckboard, she sat with her shoulders bowed in total defeat, her eyes lowered to the hands folded in her lap. The shooting, the killings, the rage and the hate – it had all weighed on her, leaving her drained and more fearful than ever.

Drift, too, didn't know what would become of the girls and was more deeply worried about that than his wounds. The

West could treat the unattached and unprotected young female in cruel ways. Girls like M'liss and Issy, uneducated in 'civilized' mores, could easily fall victim to the like of unscrupulous saloon operators and the parlour-house madams. And such practices flourished openly.

Why, hadn't he read in some newspaper that the city of Ellsworth, Kansas, made sin support the city coffers, raising $300 a month in prostitution fines?

Drift's gloom lifted when he spotted Rebecca. From a high ridge, he saw her crossing on horseback the brown waters of a river still swollen from the storm of the previous day.

She rode the pinto pony with all the assurance of the cattleman's daughter she was. Drift marvelled at her horsewoman skills, and his heart quickened as he watched.

Rebecca pulled her narrow-toed boots out of the stirrups and raised her feet to the saddle's seat, bracing her hands on the fork. It looked unsafe, but the pinto swam naturally and strongly, bringing her across the flood without a soaking.

When the pinto climbed out on the nearer shore, Drift called out. She looked up and waved excitedly before putting her mount into a lope toward them.

'You're safe,' she said, as she reached the small cavalcade. 'Thank God! I was so worried when I learned Zack had sent you out on the mountain and you hadn't returned.'

The amazing explanations were given and Drift's heart leaped anew as he noted Rebecca's quick uptake of it all; her concern at his injuries; her solicitude.

Now take it easy, cowboy, he instructed himself. This conceit just won't do at all!

Rebecca was a rich stockman and land-owner's girl. He was a saddle-tramp. No family, no home. Nothing to offer.

He had a temporary job, courtesy of her father who'd make no bones about telling her what he was. A nobody. For all that he'd discovered about his origins, he was no better off than when he'd ridden into this country.

He apologized for his bullet wound and his hurt leg. 'I'm going to be a nuisance to your pa.'

'Yes, you are a nuisance, aren't you?' Rebecca said with a smile tugging her lips. 'But a nice nuisance. I'm sorry for your wife, whoever she's going to be.'

And it was Rebecca who in due course came up with the solution for dealing with his half-sisters.

'Why, it's obvious! M'liss and Issy must go to their mother's family in Mexico, where their heritage lies.'

In the ensuing days, she enlisted her father's help. After telegraphic communication had kept the wires humming for hours, it was found that old Don Raul was long dead, but that his son, Don José, Consuela's brother and the girls' uncle, now controlled the vast Cavara empire of cattle and land. He would gladly welcome his sister's children, and they could make a

218

fresh start in life south of the Border.

Big Dutch provided transport and an escort for the two girls to El Paso, where his agent organized a meeting with their protective uncle, who was instantly captivated by Issy's vulnerability and M'liss's direct manner. It was 'a kind miracle of Heaven' that the 'pair of princesses' should at last be united with their mother's family. He would give them a new home in the palatial grandness of La Casa Cavara, freed from all care.

Back in the north, Kiliaen Van Dam's money and influence ensured that the deaths in Highgrade Pocket were hushed up. Also, a mysterious fire wiped out what was left of the ghost town but oddly failed to spread to the surrounding forests.

One day, when he was feeling particularly clear-sighted, Drift saddled up his black and rode out of the Box V, though it took every last scrap of his will power.

He was a tumbleweed and must be free to roll. It was in his blood. The bonds of matrimony were not for his kind, any more than they had been for the unfaithful man who had proven to be his father. Even it were possible, marriage would be ill-advised.

Rebecca and Big Dutch watched him leave from a gallery of their fine hacienda.

Big Dutch put his arm round his daughter's shoulder and squeezed comfortingly. 'His kind never change,' he said.

'I hope you're wrong,' Rebecca said.

But after he'd gone, she stayed alone, looking, as horse and rider dwindled to a speck.

'God speed, Drift,' she breathed, 'wherever you're headed for...'

This Large Print Book, for people
who cannot read normal print,
is published under the auspices of
THE ULVERSCROFT FOUNDATION